# HOMO SAPIEN BOB VS THE WORLD

## Episode Two

Brian Jones

ISBN-978-1-7774853-6-8 ebook
ISBN-978-1-7774853-5-1 paperback

# CONTENTS

# HOMO SAPIEN BOB
## Vs
## The World

## Episode Two

Bronx Bob
vs
Ziggy the Zebra

### Introduction

Rex here from World Mastermind Headquarters and I have to tell you that *Episode Two* is off the charts. Let me explain, so I don't lose you here!

We have a chart with the moon shining in one corner and *Episode Two* is off that chart with only half the moon dimming from the opposite corner. I know what your thinking, wholly crap, outrageous, how could you possibly accomplish all that in *Episode Two?* Volume Exactly.

The caretakers or as I like to call them the *Triple Decker Mother Earth, Mother Nature, and Father Time* had noticed recently that the world was no longer in balance. The pendulum of life has swung so far the other way leaving our World to deal with the teeter-totter effect. How do we get Homo Sapiens and Earth Entities to work together as one cohesive life?

The Triple Decker's solution to a well-balanced world is elimination. **ELIMINATION?** Yes, elimination! Homo Sapiens against Earth Entities to achieve this ambitious goal of balance. **REALLY TELL ME MORE!**

The competition in *Episode Two* consists of a Battle Royale between two captains of their industries. These Titans will have to prove to our judges which one of them brings more value to the earth. They have three rounds to convince our judges and if successful they can stay on the planet for good.

The loser will be escorted to the *MFXY Chromosome Rocket* for blast off to another world. So in the iconic words of our Rocket Man Meco BYE BYE Blue Yonder.
You might be thinking...... well that doesn't seem fair? Hey, this is planet Mother Earth flexing her muscles in the biofeedback zone of life.

In *Episode Two,* we start our journey through the Country of Troladcerlot, **Little King Bob**, King Kricket, The Queen, and *Bob the Garden Guy* with his great big hose. Also what episode would be complete if we didn't have an Elvis Impersonator, Valdi, and the Bay City Rollers to move things along.

We end up in an elevator with a horse and a mirror, a zombie who loves *Barry White* music, a timpani player along with a running synthesizer. We can't forget about the Lolulo triplets, aunt Martha, zonkey, zorse, antbee, cockhopper, or the left-handed basket weaving martial artists along with the clinically happy.

Now if that doesn't impress you we have **The Fabulous Four** who perform an unbelievable multioctavoiceagram along with the **Matilda the Singing Cow.** Matilda does more with one note than these divas can do with five octaves. **The Weeping Willows** sing their monster song Hit me with your Willow as we get whomped and stomped by the willows and waffles. There's a lot more we are just getting started!

**Bronx Bob** is one of the contestants in *Episode Two*, and he is one tough guy. He has lived his entire life, getting what he wants. In his world, everything becomes an opportunity and he manages to muscle his way into becoming a contestant. Let's just say he pulls a few strings and cashes in on some older business deals to skip the line of Bobs. He has one action in his language and that is domination and rehabilitation. Sorry, that's two actions.

**Ziggy the Zebra** is a fun-loving Zebra from the plains of the Serengeti in East Africa. He just rolls with the times and doesn't take life too seriously except when he is being chased by a lion, tiger, or crocodile. Through the years, he ends up building a massive organization AFP (all for-profit) along with his other Zebra pals and Earth Entity buddies. Ziggy eventually catches the eye of Bronx Bob and gets challenged to a winner take all event competition.

**Really!**

Bronx and Ziggy know their strengths and end up in a ferocious battle to the end of this epic adventure. Bronx Bob works between the laws that govern the world and Ziggy the Zebra works with The Laws of the Universe. Tell me something I don't know.

*Episode Two* has more twists and turns than a pretzel that has lost its way or a sheep contemplating Bungi jumping with trousers on while listening to Martha Stewart explain hopscotch on her podcast with a dog with no legs. What a drag!

Yes so sit back and enjoy the ride of this *Episode Two* extravaganza. Bronx Bob vs Ziggy the Zebra. Find out who ends up staying on planet Earth for good!

# Before you start

on your epic adventure of Homo Sapien Bob vs
the World I want to give you a **HEADS UP.**

This book was written in a style of **slang** with over expressed
**pauses**     and with many *ohhhhhs* and *ahhhhhhs* so you can
get a   feel   for the characters.
Certain words I have over **accentuated** with *italics*
to give the words more......... *meaning.*

The dialogue between characters starts with their **name**
highlighted and the conversations go off from that point. You
will notice lyrics for songs throughout Homo Sapien Bob and
this is the music I have written for each episode. On the audible
version, you can hear the songs in their entirety. When you see
Q the Music  or Q anything you know you are at a music point.

The ultimate **Homo Sapien Bob vs The World** experience is
with the book and the audible form together. You will  get a real
sense of the outrageousness of each character, plots, and themes
expressed as one complete unit.
Enjoy the ride
Cheers **Brian Jones**

# LITTLE KING BOB

*Singing and talking*

**Rex**    What a beautiful morning. I mean, the birds are singing the *Elvis impersonator* he's out early the **ducks** are protesting again and it looks like *Mother Nature's* out with her little dust devils isn't that cute ohh look it's a **glockenspiel** and a **running synthesizer.**

**I'm exactly who I should** be at this moment no one else is me who me   yes me    Ohh my goodness I mean this glockenspiel player and running synthesizer are so soothing

### From the top

I'm exactly where I should be at this moment no one else is me who me    Maybe I've got to step it up a **notch** put a little bit more **feeling** into it here we go

**Inspiration dedication what I'm feeling**    ohh my goodness Excuse me Mr. Glockenspiel player I think you hit a **wrong** note there.    I'm not *feeling* it.    Can you try it from the top?

Inspiration dedication what I'm feeling    *Ahhhh* that is friggin awful    I think I just blew up one of my **seven sacred energy centers.**

Ohh no   it's the *timpani player   little Johnny* I mean do you really have to practice the **sax** right now!

 How do you go from complete **bliss** to complete **frustration** in a **bats** eye   yet   why can the real **Batman** see   or maybe his eyes aren't the same as the real bats eyes who claim they can see where am I going with this?

> Batman has a **cape** and real bats have **wings**
> real bats don't **drive**  yet  Batman has a **car**
> It doesn't look anything a real bat would drive  **Hey**
> Batman has a **butler** the butler has a **bat**
> The bat is used to **club** the bats who are flying through the **air**
> It doesn't make any sense if real bats could drive  **Hey**

Thank goodness I'm back in my **schindler** I mean this walking to **World Mastermind Headquarters** is a great experience everyday I meet the most **intriguing** people.

I still can't figure out where this running synthesizer guy is I mean I can hear him I just can't see him.
Maybe he's running so fast he's running right past the notes he's playing into another dimension ohh that makes no sense at all. I tell you what doesn't make sense is **Frankincense** did Frank make sense or is it Frank's **scent** now that makes a lot of sense if you're into sense.

### phone rings

**Rex**    Hello Rex here    from World Mastermind Headquarters *Mother Earth  Father Time*  and *Mother Nature*   the triple-decker in one phone call  call me the **lucky** one.

**Mother Earth Mother Nature Father Time**  Phone call Talking

**Rex**    Really

**Mother Earth Mother Nature Father Time**  Phone call Talking

**Rex**    Wasn't that first competition a complete success I mean two Bobs for the price of one who would have thought      we really **knocked** it out of the ............... No that was a toilet **impersonator**       no no no not the real one     Father Time What...... really you don't  say.....ok **willow**     ok  **Aardvark** twister   twizzler blizzard.......... **Floss**   Bronx   who  what where did you say  Ziggy  no no no Iggy I said Iggy    why when ok ok ok I will get on this right now

**Rex**    Iggy   get in here

**Iggy**    Yes,   World Mastermind Rex the announcer...

**Rex**    Iggy, I just got off the phone with **the triple-decker**

**Iggy**        Triple-decker are we talking about the triple-decker hamburger place where their slogan is *triple everything* why not! or the **Lolulo Triplets**   who are triple everything.

**Rex**    Yes what a vision they are *Ahhhh*   hold on  no I'm talking about **Mother Earth   Father Time** and **Mother Nature**  and they absolutely loved everything about our first competition   **except**

**Iggy**    Yes a fabulous night Rex  The after party  who knew the **snails** could come out of their shells like that    those snails are party animals      in fact what the **hell** is a snail to begin with  are they an animal rodent or a hybrid   or   hold on Rex   did you just say   except?

**Rex**    Yes Iggy  except   never mind the snails for now.  The good news is   over the weekend we blasted the two Bobs of the planet.

**Iggy**    Bob and Booob

**Rex**        Right    we also lost another **31** Bobs at another Robert convention.

**Iggy**   Those Robert conventions are fabulous we should get legal to draw up a few more of those.

**Rex**    Great idea  can you get on that for me.


**Iggy**        You betcha   yet  my senses are telling me  we now have an upswing in the *Robert* department.

**Rex**    Yes we are gaining on Roberts but nothing to get alarmed at. We think this *Bob* to *Robert* phenomenon is just a seasonal thing where the Bobs are feeling trapped inside their name.

**Iggy**    Once you're a Bob there really isn't much more you can do with the name except for  *Bobbie*  and then you don't know if you're a boy or a girl. Not that there's anything wrong with that.

**Rex**    Yes let's be very clear on that last point.

**Iggy**    You can flip a Bob upside down he won't know if he is coming or going a very confusing name.

**Rex**    Yes I see where you're coming from  Iggy  anyways back to the triple-decker    so we lost **33** Bobs over the weekend    and another  **42** Bobs to what the planet calls the    **unnatural natural occurrences.**

**Iggy**    Are we talking about the **zombie** equation where every zombie eats his quota for the night then heads back to the zombie hut for some quiet time and *Barry White* music?

**Rex**    no no no

**Iggy**    Ohh I know what you mean      the unnatural natural occurrences    when you go to sleep with your eyes **open** and then you awake with your eyes **closed**    yet    you never wake up because your eyes are still closed.

**Rex**    Yea like that.

**Iggy**    From this stand point Rex  we are losing Bobs at a staggering rate which is good for the planet  **75** Bobs    just this past weekend alone.      Yet we have no defeats in the Earth Entity department      Mother Earth **must** be  pretty happy.

**Rex**    Yes Iggy  and  Father Time with all his astonishing wisdom seemed to be pleased as well    and let us know with some words of encouragement for our next show.

**Father Time**    I ain't got time for this crap and that's a **rap** a tap tap.

**Iggy**    Wow Father Time    who knew he could rap like that at tat

tat and Rex  I'm sorry  I still don't see the problem ?

**Rex**  The problem is   **The King of Troladcerlot** The honorable **King Kricket** with a *K* in front of ricket and the **Queen** just named their firstborn

**Iggy**   Who was just born

**Rex**  Yes  **little King Vladisloff Kricket** the **eighth** and that is *loff* after *Vladis* a *K* in front of *ricket* and *eighth* in front of an *eighth.*

**Iggy**   Ok   by the way I love the new name.

**Rex**   A Royal **farce** has exploded between the people of Trolad-cerlot and the King and Queen about the new name.

**Iggy**   Really   it sure sounds like it's a winner to me  Rex  it's got all the great qualities of what a new name should be      You know hard to **pronounce  mystery  intrigue  standoffish** yet not to **overbearing**.

**Rex**   Yes you can really **sink** your teeth into that name.

**Iggy**      Rex   can I get all this news straight  before we go any further?   I don't want to  get too confused or lose track of these **sudden** events.

**Rex**   Sure let's do a **recap**.

**Iggy**   The Honorable King Kricket with a **K** in front of ricket his first born's name is **little** King Vladisloff Kricket the eighth with **loff** after Vladis **K** before Ricket and eighth after eighth right?

**Rex**   Yes

**Iggy**      The **zombies** eat their quota each night go back to the zombie **hut** for some Barry White music.

**Rex**   Yes

**Iggy**   The unnatural natural occurrences is when you go to sleep with your eyes open    awake with your eyes closed   you never wake up because your eyes are closed   and this is not good  yet only if your name is   Bob.

**Rex**     Yes you are right  how did the zombies got involved into this?

**Iggy**    The zombies are really nice people until they get hungry.

**Rex**     Hey, they do love Barry White music

**Rex Iggy    Who doesn't**

**Iggy**    Ok I'm just a little confused on the Bob part of the King Kricket with a K in front of Ricket what am I **missing** here Rex?

**Rex**     It seems that The **H**onorable King Kricket with a **K** in front of **ricket** was never the real father of little King Vladisloff Kricket the eighth with **loff** after Vladis **K** before Ricket and eighth after **eighth**

**Iggy**    Really   then who was?

**Rex    Bob the Garden Guy**

**Iggy**    Bob the Garden Guy

**Rex**     Yes Bob the Garden Guy was brought in at spring time to help out with the **Royal Gardens** which had been showing signs of **aging** over the years. Bob the Garden Guy's specialty is *watering flowering* and *germinating*.

**Iggy**    You don't say Rex he's the real deal.

**Rex**     Bob the Garden Guy, apparently uses a special type of **hose** that is **larger** and more **sophisticated** than the Royal hose that has **special** attachments. It gets into those **hard** to reach places that the royal hose could **never** find.

**Iggy**    Really

**Rex**     Bob the Garden Guy did such a great job with the Royal Gardens he apparently caught the eye of the Queen who was very impressed with Bob the Garden Guy's new hose and what it could do.

**Iggy**   Wow   now I see   The Royal Gardens and the Queen and Little King Vladisloff Kricket that is a **loff** after Vladis **K** before Ricket and an eighth after an **eighth** are the results of Bob the Garden Guy's new hose and special attachments.

**Rex**   Yes Iggy the Royal Gardens have never looked better and the Queen is actually **smiling**.

**Iggy**   Rex, maybe the Honorable king Kricket with **K** in front of **ricket** did not give the Queen enough attention and that is why the Queen was off wandering around with Bob the Garden Guy learning about his new hose and how it worked.  They could have *accidentally* fell over a tree stump and the Queen landed on Bob the Garden Guy's new **larger** hose with the special attachments by **mistake** and then one thing lead to another.

**Rex**   You just might have a **point** Iggy   the whole country of Troladcerlot is up in arms and are demanding an explanation for this royal embarrassment.

**Iggy**   Yes it is a shame Troladcerlot was one of those up and coming destinations for travelers from around the world,  and also a hub for the long stayers.

**Rex**   Long stayers?

**Iggy**   Yes, Long stayers claim they are travel **bloggers** so they can stay longer in the country, yet they end up working in the fields as blueberry **pickers** doing the jobs that the Troladcerlots would never do.

**Rex**   At least they're not picking plums... the people of Troladcerlot are demanding that the Royal little King Vladisloff Kricket the eighth and that is a **loff** after Vladis **k** before ricket and eighth after an **eighth** have his name changed officially to **Little King Bob** and that is a **B** before an **ob** to better reflect a new wind of change in Torladcerlot.

**Iggy**   Wow these Troladcerlots are a tough crowd and demanding.

**Rex**   Tough yet fair   they have vowed that if the name does not change to Little king Bob and that is a **B** in front of an **ob** that the people of Troladcerlot will be naming their newly born kids **Bob** in honor of Bob the Garden Guy and his royal flowering.

**Iggy**   So now I understand   Bob   could spread like wildflowers across the nation of Troladcerlot in honor of the Royal flowering.

**Rex**   Wow you are a quick study Iggy   also the people of Troladcerlot   never really liked king Kricket with a **k** in front of ricket in the first place.

**Iggy**   Excuse me Rex wouldn't King Kricket with a **K** after ricket be in **second place** as opposed to first place because the people didn't like him when he was in **first** place now he has reverted back to second place in the first place?

**Rex**      Yes Iggy   you are right   I'm glad someone could finally figure out this second place in the first place stuff.

**Iggy**   Yes Rex it has puzzled me for years this second place before first place **quagmire** until I took a night class to better understand the **dynamic** exchange of energy used in just the thinking that occurs in your brain. The process of information in the second place to first place **hierarchy** has baffled Scientists (Homo Sapiens) for years.

**Rex**   Ok   I'm glad we got that out of the way.   The people found King Kricket with a **K** in front of ricket to be      **Boring   no life   a puppet      a dog without a tail.**

**Iggy**   The honorable King Kricket with a **k** before ricket sure has had a tough go of it lately, hopefully the Queen and the people of Troladcerlot can **work things out.**

**Rex**  Yes the planet and Mother Earth sure don't need an influx of new **Bob's** into the system.

**Iggy**  It's funny  Rex  I have just been handed a new video from the country of Troladcerlot.

**Rex**  Really

**Iggy**  It's their new **slogan** to get people to visit the country after the  Royal Farce.

**Rex**  These Troladcerlots don't mess around what does the slogan say?

**Iggy**  **Come to Troladcerlot for a day stay for a lifetime, were not Boring!**

**Rex**  Wow they sure want to shake things up quickly let's put it on the *big screen* and hear what they have to say.

**Rex Iggy**  Q the music

### Troladcerlot

Come to Troladcerlot for a day stay for a lifetime
Come for a lifetime plus one day  Hey

Come to Torladcerlot find more than you'll expect
That's right
Come to Torladcerlot we're an eleven out of ten
Come see our little King Bob
That's a B before an ob
Come visit the royal gardens
That's where it all started in the first place
Troladcerlot tis soaring were not boring what so ever
And if you're lucky enough you just might see Bob the garden guy
with his great big hose

Torladcerlot stay for one more day
Troladcerlot turn the planes around

Troladcerlot King and Queen are getting it on
Troladcerlot a baby Bob is on the way

Bob the Garden Guy Bob the Garden Guy
Bob the Garden Guy Love love love love
Bob the Garden Guy Bob the Garden Guy
Bob the Garden Guy a great big hose
A royal watering a royal flowering
A royal germinating nine more months
Kings not boring Queen is smiling
Countries happening Hey hey hey hey

Come to Troladcerlot for a day stay for a lifetime
Stay for a lifetime plus one day
Hey what else are you going to do with your life!

**Iggy**   Wow Troladcerlot is a happening place

**Rex**   Yes the kind of place you want to **raise** the kids.

**Iggy**   Well   They will never get bored.

**Rex**      Let's go over our show last week   **Bob vs Carl the Coal** because the triple decker

**Iggy**      Mother Earth   Father Time   and Mother Nature

**Rex**   Yes   did have a few **concerns**   going forward.

**Iggy**   Really

**Rex**   Yes   nothing major   **Father Time** was concerned that **Elvis** was looking a little thin **Mother Nature** has demanded *twizzlers, blizzards, M&M's* only the orange ones, *pop rocks, bottle caps,* and *dental floss* to be in her dressing room along with a bottle of *new coke* before the next show   and **Mother Earth** thinks the studio audience should be seated in alphabetical **order.**

**Iggy**      Alphabetical order, new coke, dental floss, bottle caps, pop rocks, M&M's orange, blizzards, twizzlers, and Elvis is looking thin. What is this a **Bustin Jeiber Ryder** contract for the next world tour?

**Rex**    Father Time just can't come to grips that Elvis is no longer with us and Mother Nature well it's that time of the year.

**Iggy**    You don't say!

**Rex**    Mother Earth felt…. some of the earth entities with their names starting with the letter *Z or Zed* depending on what part of the planet you're from  were badly behaved and we need to teach them a lesson   for the **next show.**

**Iggy**    Yes   she does have a point      the **Zombats** were dive bombing the stage at times      and I did see a standoff between a **Zonkey, Zorse**, **Zebra**, **horse**, and a **donkey** each claiming they were not the **real** father at the after party. It was a little awkward, I have to say.

**Rex**    When you have a name that starts with Z or Zed you will always be last at the **buffet** table unless you are a zombie, then you only eat when you're hungry.

**Iggy**    I think we have to talk Mother Earth out of this alphabet-ical logistical nightmare   especially when a **Zebragator** shows up and your trying to figure out

**Rex**    what were they thinking?

**Iggy**    Yes my thoughts exactly      was  the **zebra** trying to have **sex** with the **alligator**   or was the alligator trying to **eat** the zebra and then one thing lead to another **Voila** Zebragator?

**Rex**    So does the Zebragator go to the front of the studio audi-ence or to the back of the studio audience?

**Iggy**    I guess it would depend on which half they looked more like.

**Rex**    Mother Nature and her **cross** breeding experiments does she really think she's **fooling** anybody?

**Iggy**   I think the worst so far has been   the **horse fly**.

**Rex**   So what the hell does a horse and a fly see in each other in the first place? Do they see each other across a field and say **hey** I think we got a lot in **common**, meet back here at **10** and then out comes the Barry White music.

**Iggy**   Maybe the swaying of the horse's **tail** is like an aphrodisiac to the fly   I don't know   They both like to move one is running and the other is flying.

**Rex**   They both have to stop eventually for the **romance** to occur   it's not like an airplane where the plane is moving   yet the bathrooms are still standing still.

**Iggy**   How would you get them past **security** into the plane let alone into the **bathroom** and what if they wanted to have a smoke **afterwards?**

**Rex**   I'm sure **Einstein** could have figured this equation out.

**Iggy**   Let's face it our Scientists (Homo Sapiens) are still upset over the Laws of The Universe new name **AAN with two A's** and want it changed back to **Tretic Zo per en fi dite maldopobo.**

**Rex**   What a world.

**Iggy**   Yes and the poor **horses** they never seem to get a break does Mother Nature actually know what she is doing?   Now we've got different breeds of   **plants** getting together *Animals fruits vegetables tectonic plates  insects*

**Rex**   Insects more insects?

**Iggy**   Yes we just found a few new species of insects one is called **antbees** they work all day and drink all night and the next is a **cockhopper** they claim they work all day and then they drink all night.

**Rex**   Wow I feel like I'm in the dark ages.   If you were to tell me

**20** years ago we'd have antbees and cockhoppers Zorses Zonkey's and Zebragators I would never have guessed it.

**Iggy**    That's what we call **multiculturalism** in the Entity world so Rex were there any more concerns from the triple decker about our first show because I thought it was **Epic.**

**Rex**    The only other thing was an **aardvark** and a toilet apparently security found him trapped in one of the bathroom stalls for hours just flushing the toilet and watching the water swirl around looking for ants.

**Iggy**    Those aardvarks.

**Rex**    We also got word from the two Bob's this morning but the message was all broken up it went something like this **hen  b  ak 2  ear  K  ill  tim  u ck ck  ck ck then a long Ffffff      U    then another long FFFFFFFF      uuuuuuu**  at the end  can you make sense of it.

**Iggy**    I will tell you it is not Papua **New** Guinea or Pig Latin it must be one of those **subliminal** messages    read it again for me Rex

**Rex**  Ok hen b ak  2  ear  K  ill  tim  u  ck ck ck  ck  FFFFFFFF u then another long ffffffff    uuuuuuuu

**Iggy**    I think they are trying to say   **hens have 2 ears**   they like to **wear kilts** they don't know what **time** it is      they need **food** because they repeated that last part with **ffffffff**  and **uuuuuuu** twice

**Rex**    Wow that is remarkable Iggy you are a true wordsmith.

**Iggy**    The only thing that is unclear    we can ship them food and the hens with two ears    yet the **kilts** I wasn't sure if they were for the hen or the two Bob's     and **time** you're in outer space   Please.

**Rex**    If their worried about time    all they have is time    at this time

**Iggy** I hope they get their **priorities** straight because this will be a long journey to a destination

**Rex** they will never get to?

**Iggy** Yes now you're getting it Rex just like those poor horses.

**Rex** Now let's get on with the first show after thoughts I thought it went *extremely* tremendous. We could **nit pic** it apart dissect it to the external extremities give it some **fodder for the flow** or **ginder for the gander** yet in the end the show had all the elements of a finely tuned swiss

**Iggy** **cheese?**

**Rex** No no no

**Iggy** **chocolate?**

**Rex** No no no

**Iggy** oh I got it a finely tuned **Schindler.**

**Rex** Yes they make fabulous elevators

**Iggy** They truly are the go to elevators when you need an elevator.

**Rex** World Mastermind Headquarters has **17** schindlers and I never get that feeling of being trapped inside a schindler there like your home **away** from home.

**Iggy** Yes I know what you mean the building next door went with a cheaper brand of elevator. I keep thinking please this is the message you're sending your employees and customers?

**Rex** Lord take me home back to my schindler take me home to that place inside my schindler.

**Iggy** Rex you know what I'm thinking

**Rex** yes my thoughts exactly

**Rex Iggy**   Q the music

## Elevator

In love with my elevator take me where I want to go
Waits for me before it ever close the door
Safe inside it raise me to the sky
teaches me to be greater than yesterday
Time to access my life

In Love with my elevator place I want to be
judge myself the mirror it don't lie
Step inside and take a ride
There's no place left to hide
Put away the mask find the truth
And breath…………
Put yourself at ease…….

Lifts me up to higher ground
view life from a different mound
Clear the noise and all that sound
Elevator

Can go through life with blind eyes
One day you're going to realize
One shot to master life
Elevator

**Rex**   Love that song I have some of my best thoughts inside our schindler elevators.

**Iggy**   Yes they have sure **fine tuned** the elevator experience to another level. I don't know how the competition can ever catch up in the elevator race.

**Rex**   it's really just a one horse race.

**Iggy**   you know   I just thought of something?

**Rex**   Ok Hit me

**Iggy**   You know how the **horse race tracks** around the world are having a hard time attracting people back to the track?

**Rex**   Yes  so they decided to add *casinos, entertainment,* and *free parking* on Tuesday evenings.

**Iggy**   Don't forget the two foot long **hot dogs** for the price of one only after 10 pm on every other Wednesday in February.

**Rex**   Yes

**Iggy**   The Homo Sapiens have been given a **sweet heart** of a deal at the horse race track   yet   the **poor** horses which the bloody thing is named after are still chasing after a destination they will never get to.

**Rex**   Yes those poor horses they don't know if their coming or going.

**Iggy**   So   what if the Horse Race was more about the winning horse and his **athleticism**, and not about the *90 pound jockey, cigar smoking owner, betting wager ticket daily double trifecta,* and the **stud fees**.

**Rex**   Don't forget the *trumpets, fancy hats, lipstick, eyeshadow, watch sponsors,* and two pairs of **shoes** just in case you step in

**Iggy**   never mind that **crap**   what about the three types of *sunglasses, safety pins, bobby pins* and the mini **air pump** for those outfit malfunctions.

**Rex**   You forgot about the well-cut **dress** that falls below the knees

**Iggy**   the revealing **neckline**

**Rex**   and the **personal trainer** who lives in the pool Cabana with the **pool boy** with the great tan.

**Iggy**   impish **grin**

**Rex**   and **speedo**

**Iggy**   What does the poor horse **get?**

**Rex**   **Exhaustion**

**Iggy**   **stick** in the side

**Rex**   oats

**Iggy**   **brushing**

**Rex**   **flowers** and a **pat** on the back

**Iggy**   more **vitamin injections.**

**Rex**   It doesn't seem worth it for the horse.

**Iggy**   What if the winning horse   got to spend a night in the are you ready for it   **The Schindler Stall**   all the best features that a schindler elevator offers   yet designed for the horse in mind **time alone   mirror   music**   and that feeling of never really leaving home.

**Rex**   Yes we could broadcast live   over the world wide web   and call it **Schindler's Horse for a night**   as can't miss entertainment.

**Iggy**   A horse in the Schindler stall   would have the same opportunity and benefits as Homo Sapiens in the schindler elevator you know   look at themselves in the **mirror,** fix their **hair,** check to see if anything is caught in their **teeth,** and practice **smiling.**

**Rex**   Yes and they could listen to some **music** and practice a couple of **dance moves** in front of the surround mirror imagery.

**Iggy**   In the schindler stall they can scratch themselves, **fart** and pretend when the door opens   **hey**   that wasn't me look on their **face.**

**Rex Iggy**   *hahaha* never done that before   **right**

**Iggy**   Those Schindler Elevators their just like home.

**Rex**    Now before this episode goes **sideways** Iggy lets close the door on the elevator and the horse.

**Iggy**    and the impish grinned speedo wearing pool boy.

**Rex    Bob vs Carl the Coal**    Was there anything you thought we needed to improve on?

**Iggy**    I don't know Rex I think it went fabulous    maybe a little more **juggling** to keep some of the crowd entertained like the *orangutans, prey mantis, dolphins,* and the **dust** particles.

**Rex**    They seemed a little distracted I noticed.

**Iggy**    Some of the Homo Sapiens who came in groups seemed bewildered by the event. The clinically **happy**, severely **frustrated**, and the *left handed basket weaving martial artists,* seemed to need more entertainment than just the show itself.

**Rex**    Wow fabulous observation Iggy. We will have to address these issues before our next    Competition.

**Iggy**    You betcha Rex    now the only other issue I found which was not an issue at all was

**Rex**    the **after party**?

**Iggy**    Yes don't touch that event that was absolutely fabulous.

**Rex**    The crowd that stayed for the after party were sure treated to the **event** of the year. Who would have thought you would ever see **lizards spiders** and **ants** forming conga lines.

**Iggy**    How about those **thunder clouds** not raining on the group from the Homo Sapiens called

**Rex Iggy**    the society who carry **umbrellas** because they don't make **coats** small enough for our **chihuahua's.**

**Iggy**    Yes I don't think there was a **dry eye** in the house that was a very touching moment.

**Rex**   Mother Nature was actually   **smiling.**

**Iggy**   You know this is when the best of the planet works together for the common good Homo Sapiens getting along with Earth Entities and vice versa.

**Rex**   Your right Iggy

**Iggy**   The entertainment was A+ with a couple more pluses.

**Rex**   We had no idea **The Fabulous Four** were going to show up and dazzle the audience like they did.

**Iggy**   Yes *Delean Selon  Starbra  Bryson  Crya Mary  Aristean Co agulary* they were singing like **Diva's**  Each one trying to out Diva the other.

**Rex**   It was like watching **Circus Solei** meets **monster truck** meets the **penguins** in happy feet.

**Iggy**   I think the magic moment was when The Fabulous Four invited **Matilda the Singing Cow** on to the stage to measure her greatness against The Fabulous Four.

**Rex**   Yes she held her own against The Fabulous Four if not stole the show she did not disappoint.

**Iggy**   The Fabulous Four were **stretching** every octave out of the five octave range with sweeping scales of graciousness.

**Rex**   Matilda the Singing Cow was hitting the notes in between the notes, she was **scaling** between **each** individual **note.**

**Iggy**   If I didn't hear it with my own two ears I wouldn't have believed it.

**Rex**   I don't think **Mozart**, **Beethoven**, or the **Bay City Rollers** could have figured those melodies out.

**Iggy**   She's that great even the Fabulous Four were **bowing** their heads after her vocal **extraordinaire** performance.

**Rex**   Let's face it  Matilda the Singing Cow is who all the greats measure themselves against.

**Iggy**   We managed to get a snippet of The Fabulous Four and Matilda the Singing Cow on their encore performance.

**Rex Iggy**   Q the snippet

### The Fabulous Four
### w/ Matilda the Singing Cow

Bumpum Bumpum Bumpum BumpumI've been
don't you know   I've been don't you know
I've been don't you know
Sit Downnnnnnnnn
Pub a doom da Dum Pub a doom da Dum
Pub a doom da Dum Pub a doom da Dum
Ohhhhhhh  Yea Yea Yea
Oh Oh Shake your body Now
Oh Oh Shake your body Now
Madora a  ah aha ah
Madora a  ah aha ah
FU FU FU
FU FU FU
The fella's know I'm a dine
I gotta meet with the line
They can't believe a girl as
cheap as me is sick with the rhyme
Oh Oh Oh Oh
Mo Moo Mooo
Mo Mooo Mo
Moo Moo
Mo Mo Mo MO MO

**Iggy**   What a truly remarkable performance I think that will go down in the history books right up there with *Elvis  The Beatles Michael Jackson*  and  **Twisted Sister.**

**Rex**   A performance for the ages.

**Iggy**   The Fabulous Four were fabulous.

**Rex**   Yet the notes that Matilda the Singing Cow was hitting left many people **scratching** their heads.

**Iggy**   A talent like hers only comes around once in your lifetime so treasure it when you can.

**Rex**   The next moment for me was when the **Weeping Willows** hit the stage, the party seemed to **elevate** to another level.

**Iggy**   Oh my goodness are the Weeping Willows even capable of **writing** a bad song?

**Rex**   The crowd became **unwound** when the Weeping Willows came out with their monster hit **Hit me with your Willow.**

**Iggy**   The followers of the weeping willows came out in huge numbers and brought their **willows** and **waffles**.

**Rex**   Yes it was a sea of willows and waffles everywhere.

**Iggy**   What a sight   what a world.

**Rex**   Those willows **hurt** when you get whipped by the willow and then whomped by the waffle.

**Iggy**   Yes it's the one two combination that makes the whipping and whomping so effective.

**Rex**   Yes it's like getting stung by a **wasp** and then kissed by a **worm** at the same time and then you get to **wallow** in your web of wowness.

**Iggy**   Then at the end of the song when the waffle wompers gather up all the stray waffles

**Rex**   and perform their final whomping.

**Iggy**   Whomping and stomping on all the waffles as the wil-lowers are whipping the wompers.

**Rex**    Yes it was a sight to witness from afar

**Iggy**    You know what I'm thinking

**Rex Iggy**    Yes    Q the music

### Hit me with your Willow

Hit me with your willow make it short and sweet
Hit me with your willow like a dog needs treats
There's no denying this truth inside of me
Ring that bell saliva hits my feet

I'm yours your willow intoxicates
I'm yours you're willow i can't wait
You reach me like no one else can
Defenseless this is my last stand

Whip me - whip me with your willow
Teach me - teach me with your willow
Touch me - touch me with your willow
Love me - love me with your willow

Hit me with your willow make it short and sweet
Whomp me with the waffle like a dog needs treats
Hit me with your willow there's no retreat
Whomp me with the waffle just repeat

Willow waffle willow    waffle willow waffle
Willow waffle willow    willow waffle waffle willow

Waffle willow waffle    willow waffle willow
Waffle willow waffle    waffle willow willow waffle

Willow waffle willow    waffle willow waffle
Willow waffle willow    willow waffle waffle willow

Waffle willow waffle    willow waffle willow
Waffle willow waffle    waffle willow willow waffle

Willow waffle waffle willow    Waffle willow willow waffle
Willow waffle waffle willow    waffle willow waffle

**Rex**    Like wow    Hit me with your Willow    could there be a bigger song in the world right now?

**Iggy**    Yes    no I mean no    it's a **monster** of a hit    the weeping willows and the whipping and whomping and stomping at the end with the waffles    it's the whole package.

**Rex**    Tell me who has more fun the **whippers** the **whompers** or the **stompers**?

**Iggy**    Let's see In the whipping your two feet are planted and you have arm action and the whomping and stomping your feet are moving up and down so I'm wavering on the whipping or the whomping.

**Rex**    Yes it is a tough one each one has their own unique style and athleticism.

**Iggy**    I just haven't figured out the difference between the whomping and the stomping.

**Rex**    That easy just take the **WH** and exchange it for the **ST**

**Iggy**    Brilliant observation.

**Rex**    I think we can wrap this after party review up and get on with our next order of business.

**Iggy**    **The next show.**

**Rex**    Do you have any ideas or concerns of how we can make the next show a better success than this first fine offering?

**Iggy**    I do have a few concerns about several messages that have been left on my phone over the weekend claiming that the first Bob and the bonus Bob BOOOOB were a joke.

**Rex**    A Joke    Really?

**Iggy**     Yes a joke and an **embarrassment** to the foundation of Bob's that represent Bob's around the world.

**Rex**     Foundation of Bob's

**Iggy**     All I know from the message he calls himself **Bronx**.

**Rex**     That's funny when I was talking to the triple Decker

**Iggy**     Mother Earth Father Time and Mother Nature

**Rex**     Yes   they mentioned someone had contacted them after the show who was very **adamant** to find out who was responsible for the competitors in the competition. He also went by name of Bronx. I wonder if it was the same Bronx?

**Iggy**     Yes that must be Bronx.   **Bronx Bob** he claims he always gets what he wants.

**Rex**     Well that's great.

**Iggy**     Great   he told me   my **wife** was asking for a **divorce** if I did not make him the next Bob and something about a **car, false teeth**, and a **wig**.

**Rex**     Wow that is rough   I never  knew you were even married Iggy.

**Iggy**     I'm not   Bronx claims he knows who   my future wife is and she will be asking for a divorce.

**Rex**     Wow that didn't last long  yet I think in times like this  we need to talk with the **oracle** of wisdom our amazing truth of the **seeker** of all that is right and wrong in the world.

**Iggy**     **Father Time**

**Rex**     Yes Father Time we need to get him on the Father of Time special hotline to see what he makes of this delicate situation.

**Iggy**     The last time we called him he just yelled and screamed

**Rex**  Yes he did  yet the words he used between the profanity

**Iggy**  were **words of wisdom**.

**Rex**  Ok let's get Father Time on the line to seek his wisdom

**Father Time**  Father Time here and I ain't got time for this crap so start talking and if this is Bronx Bob.  hey no hard feelings it's in the mail.

**Rex**  Father Time its Rex and Iggy from World Mastermind Headquarters and we need your **worldly** wisdom for a moment.

**Father Time**  Rex and Iggy I told you last time I ain't got time for this crap.

**Iggy**  Father Time I got a message from Bronx Bob.

**Father Time**  Bronx Bob give that man whatever he wants and make sure we never had this **conversation**. I ain't got time for this **crap** so leave me alone so I can concentrate on my **time through space** conundrum.

**Rex**  Wow another example of Father Times relentless wisdom

**Iggy**  and truth  he must know Bronx Bob as well.

**Rex**  I think we need to listen to that message **now**  Iggy.

**Iggy**  Yes the Bronx Bob guy has a lot of **demands** so you better get out a pen, paper, and a good thesaurus cause he kind of goes off in a few area's for long extended periods of time.

**Rex**  Good idea  your future **pretend** wife  is at stake here maybe it's one of the  Trolulo triplets?

**Iggy**  *Ahhhhhh* Rex we definitely have to save my marriage because their **yummy**.

**Rex**  Right

**Iggy**  What are we waiting for!

**Rex** This is probably a good time to warp this episode up and have a listen to Bronx Bob and his message.

**Iggy** It's more like many messages that are all strewn together like a **Wassily Kandinsky** composition **or** my **nephew's** rendition of the little **school house** drawn after two glasses of **coke** and **cheezies** with finger **paint**.

**Rex** We will get to the bottom of this Bronx Bob whoever he is?

**Rex Iggy Q the message**

# SLOTHING

**Bronx Bob**     Iggy do not **hang up**! This is Bob     **Bronx Bob** on the message line of truth  I speak    I'm here to fill your head with some insights  who's insights?  my insights  **I** know  **you** know **why** I'm calling.   I watched that travesty of a show     you and Rex put on with Mother Earth   Mother Nature   and Father time it was like watching a **hula hoop** dancing around the waist of an **iguana** who was doing **pushups** to the sounds of **Valdi** through a **stethoscope**.  It was weak man, I mean weak.   At least Valdi's got some coolness.

Don't tell me this is the best  solution that **World Mastermind Headquarters** people came up with to solve *overpopulation, climate change, pollution, poverty, extinction,*  and the ever popular **nail fungus** yellow toe disease   I mean please  a competition? You're going to need a few more  Rockets  contests and brain cells to figure this one out.    I got one word for you   repeated three different ways   *Cooperation   Coagulation*  and   *Crap* as I like to call it the **CCC** approach.

Your first contestant who lost and got blasted off the planet   **Bob** from Bakersville California I mean,  please    he's a plumber   no one likes **plums**  or  in its royal form  **Prunes**   in fact  Plums and Prunes    were voted as the worst fruit of all time if you have   **hemorrhoids**    and the best fruit of all time if you had **constipation**  Pick your poison   Yes for the *believers, disbelievers* and *nonbelievers* there high in antioxidants **check**  help out with the heart  **check**  lowers your blood pressure  **check**     one tablespoon of this  **Potent of Content**  will relieve constipation

31

and tickle the hemorrhoids **check**   hey here's a tip from the Food Almanac for stupid people   Stop eating crap   It's called **CICO** CRAP IN CRAP OUT   so to sum up relief in **six simple steps**

1. Take one tablespoon of plums or prunes
2. Go to the Home Depot with your credit card
3. Buy a toilet in a box
4. Open the box and sit on the toilet and wait for the relief
5. Once you are finished, tape the box backup and puncture a hole in the top
6. Take the toilet back into Home Depot and complain profusely that you were sold a used toilet. They will never open the box and they might even up your limit on your card for the inconvenience. Side note you can do this in their serene parking lots.

**Next**   blastoff participant   **Bob** bonus Bob   International rap Superstar   **Boooob**   he's a **superstar** of   hmmmm   let me repeat that a superstar of what?   Hey as a Bob I was offended for every *BOB BOB* and *BOB* out there.   He should have been arrested for crimes against people named   Bob   hopefully you blasted his **ego** along with his alter ego   and a box of **eggo's** to feed all those egos.   Good ridden

Finally some common sense came to the show    **Carl the Coal** was the winner and got to stay on the planet for good. You got it right!   That boy got some **real** potential packed inside him.   He offers a great deed for the planet, equilibrium and a delicate balancing act for Mother Earth Mother Nature and Father Time. Side Note what the hell does Father Time do anyways. Since he tied his **anchor** to space it's like we can't get rid of him. It takes Time to move through space I mean please it takes time to move through his crap. At least he's entertaining in a not so quantum way.

You see **Iggy**   I'm a very **reasonable man** or should I say I'm a real reasonable Bob Bronx Bob and I always   I mean always   get what

I want. When I see an opportunity Iggy I always take it and to be honest no one ever says no hmmm if you know what I mean.

I am what you call the **Business Aficionado** if I see a business opportunity that is to my liken then I got to know it.

So let me give you a quick **Bitty**
On why I'm such a strong **Gritty**
So you can be more with the **Witty**
Without suffering with the **Pity**
If you want to see your **Kitty**
You better listen to this **Ditty**

**Bronx Bob**          **Q the Ditty**

**I'm your next Bob**


Iggy you better listen to me if you know what's best
I get what I want cause I'm Bronx Bob
I get what I need cause I'm Bronx Bob
I take what I need cause I'm Bronx Bob
I do what I want cause I'm Bronx Bob

I know you don't want a horse's head in your bed
I know you need a tongue if you wanna be fed
Don't wanna go swimming with a piece of lead
No is not the answer that needs to be said

Iggy I'm your next Bob
I'm your next Bob
Iggy I'm your next I'm your next

The last two Bob's couldn't clean my shoes
Carl the Coal he packs a ton of value
I can spell out what you should do
Open your ears let me give you the news

Iggy I'm your next Bob
I'm your next Bob

> Iggy I'm your next I'm your next
> Bob I'm your next Bob I'm your Next Bob
> I'm your next Bob I'm your next Bob

**Bronx Bob**     So Iggy let me be **Frank** with you     hold on I mean **Bob** with you     I am your next Bob for this competition     I need to represent all the     Bob's     out there     and give the name the **credibility** and **respect** it needs.     Bob is a **strong** name, a **foundational** name, a name that is based on simplicity     yet     It's circles can be complex with a single dash of a straight line leading to infinity     yet     only in its capital form     First letter English.     We even have our own day     **Bob Day**     sept 17th. This is a day where all the Bob's around the world     thank their lucky stars they were never called **Leonard Tim** or **Sandy** I mean please.

The fact you're blasting a Bob off the planet to relieve some pressure   is well let's say   *cute comical* and *crazy*   but why Bob?   You could have picked any other weak named   Homo Sapien for the competition   yet you picked Bob.

Let's face it     **Earth Entities** they are everywhere     ohh look I just stepped on some **grass** with **ants** and **caterpillars**     with **daffodils**   with a **wasp** ready to sting me   I mean please   take your pick which one would you like to blast off the planet first? Hey why not all of them   we still have replacements for these five How about **astro turf** for grass, **termites** which are ant look likes, **butterflies** or caterpillars   a **society** who can't decide who they want to be   pick one, Daffodils or **peeping toms** hey they only come out once in year, and finally **hornets** never got the same notoriety as wasps. I'm just getting started.

**Apples** we have **7500** different types of   apples   do we need them all?   Hey I got a great idea let's pick one or two apple types and stick with that   and be happy.   I know I know   **Mary** from Slovakia with the **varicose veins**   has twenty types of apple trees in her backyard.   She bakes hundreds of **pies** each year and finally when her family, friends and enemies get sick of her pies   she hands them out to the **homeless** frozen. Then gets an award for **BEST CITIZEN EVER** I mean Please! Let's take Mary with her varicose veins, family, friends, enemies, apple trees, frozen pies, homeless and her awards and put them on a big rocket and clear out the congestion.

This is balancing the planet and congestion Bronx Bob style.

So Iggy I need to step in and be like a **traffic cop** and make sure the strong survive and the weak are eliminated off this planet.

Of course my plan is for **self-preservation** of a few essentials which we won't get into here. I want to work with Mother Earth, Mother Nature and especially Father Time on their quest for **equilibrium** on the planet.

The competition I realize now is a great way to accomplish this task and that is why I am stepping in.

I will be by on **Monday** to talk with you and Rex and trust me anytime will be a good time for you. I have one request **be there** when I **get there.**

So Sleep tight
And do what's right
Don't let the bugs bite *Ooh yea Ooh yea Ooh yea Ooh yea*

**Rex** Iggy Is Bronx Bob is he done is he finally finished?

**Iggy** No Rex, he's got one more I think you're going to love this one.

**Bronx Bob** Hi Rex I know you're listening to this message so to make this easy to understand **I** will be The Bob for the next **competition** I hope we have established that as we move forward. I have gone ahead and handpicked my **competitor**. I need a strong competitor one who will bring out my best. I have added one more **judge** because I can! I had a quick talk with Mother Earth, Mother Nature and Father Time. Let's say you'll be getting a call from them really soon....... So I hope you find this to your liking   see you both real real soon.  Bob  Bronx Bob

So sleep tight
And do what's right
Don't let the bugs bite *Ooh yea   Ooh yea   Ooh yea   Ooh yea*

**Rex**   He has to be finished now?

**Iggy**   Well there are a few more **Ooh yea's  sleep tights** and a couple of swear words nothing to get alarmed at.  He did tell me I would get my car back,  one Lolulo triplet,  Tiddy the Kitty,  my Grandmother's false teeth, and Aunt Martha's wig.

**Rex**   Well that's great news about the car, triplets, Tiddy the Kitty, false teeth, wig and how's Aunt Martha?   Excuse me did you say Monday?

**Iggy**   Yes

**Rex**   That's today   let's call security.

**Iggy**   Well that sounds great   Rex   but   World Mastermind Headquarters security is  Bronx Bob's security company called **BS Security**   their slogan   **Because WE CAN**.

**Rex**   *Ohhhhh* really    I didn't know that    how do you  feel about this **sudden** turn of events   Iggy.

**Iggy**   Well as in the eternal words of Father Time   He does have that Time and Space **Newtonian** thing going for him   plus his un-canny **Cranel of knowledge**  plus his words of a finely tuned **word-smith**.   Give that man what he wants.   So I'm with Father Time.   Let's give this man what he wants.   We need to get this show   out of the **way,** out of the **hopper**, and into a show **stopper** it will be.

**Rex**   Well I guess it doesn't hurt to open our basket of listening skills and listen to what he has to say.     The big man upstairs gave us two **ears** and one **mouth** so we should follow the **quantity** ratio. *Duhhhhh*

**Iggy**   I think we need  to do more than just listen  we need to supply **cheese** and saltine **crackers**. You know the ones that suck up all the saliva in your mouth so we can't listen to him talk so much.

**Rex** Great idea Bronx Bob has what you call **diarrhea of the mouth** it's as common as the flu yet it's in the mouth.

**Iggy** We should give him some **beef jerky** and let him chew on that for a while.

**Rex and Iggy** it's a great source of **protein**.

**Iggy** Hey side note here Beef jerky Did you know that **7-eleven** recently offered **insurance** policies for people who eat Jerky?

**Rex** Yes **The Eat Jerky Die Rich Life policy.**

**Iggy** 7-eleven has figured out if they can hook people long enough in buying their beef Jerky they can also offer them life Insurance.

**Rex** Yes it is a **win win** situation for all **three** parties involved.

**Iggy** The *seller* the *eater* and the *waiter* are all compensated.

**Rex** Wow what a world we live in!

**Iggy** Did you also know my **Dad** was a nuclear scientist janitor's **assistant**?

**Rex** Really I didn't know that. Where are we going with this Iggy?

**Iggy** **Factoid 1** Every scientists building in the world has a 7-eleven store parked on either side that is open **24**hrs a day **365** days a year. **Factoid 2** Scientists (Homo Sapiens) can get a quick fix for their beef jerky consumption in minutes when the **equations** get too complicated

**Rex** That's startling yet it makes sense when you realize you can be in two places at the same time in the quantum world.

**Iggy**   Yes the Scientists (Homo Sapiens) love eating beef jerky they say it's an **aphrodisiac** for the mind. They might know a lot about science   yet   the mouth becomes the **black hole** for the jerky and the toilet becomes the **vortex** for the deposit.

**Rex**   *Ahhh* it's too bad the Scientists (Homo Sapiens) couldn't have seen the world through your Dad's eyes.

**Iggy**   Studies recently have shown that the **coagulation** between the jerky   the higher intelligent mind  and dust from the chalk used to write their equations causes   **SMB.**

**Rex**   Yes **Sudden Mind Burst**

**Iggy**   Scientists (Homo Sapiens) today when they get SMB have to run to the nearest 7-eleven store and  buy some **starbursts** or **skittles**, lay on their backs outside the stores and wait for the relief to show up.

**Rex**   **Factoid 3**   This must explain why most Scientists (Homo Sapiens) are **cross eyed**. Watching the stars, the road while waiting for relief seems to confuse their eyes and they end up losing track of where they are in the **cosmos.**

**Iggy**   Nice to meet you **Mr. Scientist**  hey  you got **Marty Feldman cosmos eyes.**

**Rex**   The sad part is these Scientists (Homo Sapiens) are supposed to be our brightest minds.

**Iggy**   Yes let me remind you these Scientists (Homo Sapiens) are the same people who gave us **Tretic Zo per en fi dite maldopobo** as the new name for **The Laws of the Universe.**

**Rex**   Well this sure sounds like it's going to be an interesting week.   Hey I'm getting another call from the triple decker.

**Rex**   Hello  Mother Earth Mother Nature  and Father time   Ok ohhh yeaaaa really yet but what   I    think oh it doesn't matter give who are you sure ok I will get right on it. How can we do that!

Ohhh I get it.

**Iggy**   Tell me we have some options?

**Rex**   **NO**   apparently Bronx Bob is on his way over  and he will be the next  **Bob**   for the competition.

**Iggy**   Really   this guy comes in here   like the **eye** of the storm yet   we have to realize that a Homo Sapien (Bronx Bob) or an Earth Entity will  blast off the planet.  This has to be our focus.

**Rex**   Yes Iggy you are right my only concern is who is going to be the competition   you know   the **Earth Entity**?

**Iggy**   Bronx Bob said earlier   he had handpicked his competitor for the competition.   I wonder what it will be?   a **dragonfly**   an **oak tree**   or how about a **Kangaroo**.

**Rex**   Why would he pick a **tough** competitor and risk  getting blasted off the planet.   A dragonfly oak tree and a kangaroo let's face it   that's tough competition.

**Iggy**   Yes he will probably pick something safe like a   **sloth** no offense to the sloths out there slothing.

**Rex  Slothing**   are you thinking what I'm thinking Iggy

**Iggy**   Yes

**Rex and Iggy**   Q the slothing

### I'm a Sloth

I'm a Sloth hanging upside down inside a tree
I'm a sloth camouflage so you don't see me
I'm a sloth 3x stronger than a human being
I'm a sloth one armed pushup with such ease

Don't believe everything you read about me
Don't believe you call me  Lazy
Believe me Love Avocados thank me
Believe me 100 foot fall don't faze me

I'm a sloth Hey baby why don't you come
over here and give me some love
I'm a sloth why don't you come over here
I've got some great hands
I'm a sloth hey baby don't worry I'm the king of this branch
I'm a sloth hey baby come over here and i will show you my life

I'm a sloth Nine million years it's who I be
I'm a sloth sleeping upside down hanging from a tree
I'm a sloth I'm a carnivore of the leaf
I'm a sloth thirty days till I relieve

Colored blind don't hold that against me
Sense of smell with one hell of a memory
Hit the ground I move at turtle speed
In the water I'm your speed boat at sea

I'm a sloth yea yea yea I'm a sloth yea yea yea

**Iggy**     Slothing you got to love it. It's that kind of slow move **forward** as your **hips** are moving **backward**, your **feet** are pointed **sideways** and you got your **arms** up in the **air.**

**Rex**  Don't forget your **eyes** are relaxed staring forward with your **tongue** hanging out   and every so often you hear that   **crack**   in your **back**   then you know it's time to change **positions.**

**Iggy**   It's almost that **zombie contortionist** type of move   but your **dancing.**

**Rex**   Let's face it   sloths   have had such a bad rap over the years. The world's laziest animal   I mean please.

**Rex**   If you can move like that you're not **lazy.**

**Iggy**   Yes   so many individual moving parts

**Rex**   in different directions

**Iggy**   while getting your **groove** on

**Rex**    while maintaining your **balance**.

**Iggy**    sticking your **tongue** out

**Rex**    **staring** forward

**Iggy**    Listening for the **crack**.

**Rex**    Now get a whole room slothing at the same time   Wow.

### Knock knock knock

**Rex**   Hey can you wait a minute    we're slothing.

**Iggy**    Now Rex you almost have it    move your hips **backward** before you move **forward**    point your toes to the **side**    put your hands in the **air**    stare **forward**    put your tongue **out**    and then listen for the **crack.**

### Effects   crack

**Iggy**    Now change position and start all over.

### Knock knock knock

**Rex**    Hey please give us a minute.

### Knock knock knock

**Iggy**    Some people here at *World Mastermind Headquarters* have no manners!

### Door busts open

**Rex and Iggy**    Who the hell are you?

**Bronx Bob**    Bob   Bronx Bob

**Rex and Iggy**    Bob    Bronx Bob ohhh *well...*

**Bronx Bob**    Niiiiiice    is this what you **Boys** do in your spare time?

**Rex and Iggy**   Well no   no well we

**Bronx Bob   Quiet!** Before we get down to business   Let me first say     you Boys have got this **slothing dance** all wrong   I own many slothing clubs   so I do know   a thing or two about slothing and what I see   your slothing has no **flow**   it's **dysfunctional.**

**Iggy**   Dysfunctional slothing flow *I* knew it!

**Bronx Bob**   Yes Iggy   so if you don't mind let me give you both a quick lesson on the **fine** art of slothing.

### Q the slothing

**Bronx Bob**     Now before we start   Rex and Iggy     get your feet firmly on the **ground** and slightly bent at the **knees.**  These moves aren't natural for the **body** so this is where the flow comes in.   Lead with your left **foot** forward   then move your **hips** backwards    feel the flow   do it a couple of times so you can get that natural rhythm going.

**Rex**  Bronx Bob   my **ass** keeps going up in the air at this stage.

**Bronx Bob**     Squeeze your ass **cheeks**   Rex    that is the **secret sauce**   and that starts the natural flow of the movement.

**Iggy**  They never taught   flow and secret sauce   at the slothing clubs.   So when do I start squeezing my ass cheeks?

**Bronx Bob**   You squeeze right from the beginning   and this prevents the ass from tilting in the air   and starts the flow.

**Rex**  See Iggy look at Bronx Bob's ass it never goes in the air.

**Iggy**  He has great form   you could bounce a **quarter** off his ass.

**Rex**  It's straight as an **arrow.**

**Bronx Bob**  The real secret is to get this first move down properly then    you can go on to the rest of the slothing. I think you boys are doing great.

**Rex**  I think I've got the first move down with flow.

**Iggy**  Yes the **clenching** of the ass muscles is a real game changer.

**Bronx Bob**  Now let's combine the feet pointing out   as we swing our arms in the air.

**Rex**  This is where most people have a hard time and end up with dysfunctional slothing flow.

**Bronx Bob**  If you can learn the natural flow from the start   you naturally go into these next moves.

**Iggy**  Yes my ass is now in the flow   my feet are pointed   and my hands are in the air.

**Rex**  I can feel it   it's almost as natural as **breathing**.

**Bronx Bob**  Now let's add the last two moves to the sloth.   When you have **control** over your ass it **lowers** your head and now you can have that **relaxed** stare as you stick your tongue out and wait for the crack.

**Iggy**  Wow Bronx Bob that is amazing   I feel so relaxed.

**Rex**  Yes and the final crack  sounds like **popcorn** popping at the movies.

**Iggy**  Most people have this look of **desperation** like they're con- stipated and end up like zombies and get **startled** by the crack.

**Bronx Bob**  Yes the magic lies in mastering each move before you head to the next move.

**Rex**  Yes the whole sloth is like *poetry in motion*   amazing.

**Bronx Bob**  Well there you go  Boys  The Sloth.

**Rex**  Thanks Bronx Bob

**Iggy**  Yes thanks Bronx Bob.

**Bronx Bob**  Now Rex and Iggy let's get down to business and dis- cuss why I'm here.

**Iggy**  Ok Bronx Bob we

**Bronx Bob**  Hold on Rex and Iggy call me Bob  Bronx is my working name and seeing we've had a **moment** of slothing together let's forget the Bronx title.

**Rex**  Bob  this competition is a process to eliminate Homo Sapiens or Earth Entities off the planet for good.

**Iggy**  We are helping Mother Earth with her **global goal** of balancing the planet  for its long term health.

**Iggy**  Why would you  volunteer to help  and risk  being blasted off the planet for good is puzzling?

**Bronx Bob**  You see boys  I have always gotten what I want in life. When I see an opportunity I have no hesitation and go in and dominate industries.  My **tentacles** are long and wide and  sometimes I play **above** the law and  **below** it.

So when I saw that first show  last week  and  you were only picking Bob's  and an Earth Entity,  that was my **clue** to step in. I wanted to get your attention fast  so that is why I took the measures I did.

 I found out quickly **Iggy**  you were the one responsible for the **competitors**  so I chose  a *Lolulo triplet, a car,* your *grandma's false teeth* and *Aunt Martha's wig*  to let you know I meant business.

**Iggy**  Yes you got my attention quickly the Lolulo triplets their yummy.

**Rex**  Forget about the triplets  **yummy**  Iggy  Bob there has to be more than just being a competitor  this could go terribly wrong for you.

**Bronx Bob**  Yes of course.

**Iggy**  You also told us you **handpicked** your competition?

**Bronx Bob**   Yes my competitor is someone I have known for years yet we come from two different backgrounds.  He is head of an organization that I would  love to get to know better   if you know what I mean.

**Rex**   No not really.

**Iggy**   So this is for financial gain in the end   Bob?

**Bronx Bob**   Yes of course   my competitor and I   have worked out an **agreement** between the two of us   that will **benefit** the winner   and **devastate** the loser.

**Rex**   Does Mother Earth, Mother Nature, and Father Time understand  this agreement completely?

**Bronx Bob**   Yes   Father Time owes me a few **favors** over the years and I'm cashing in **big time.**

**Rex**   It sounds like a lot to risk   Bob   when you have so much.

**Iggy**    We need to know who the competitor will be!

**Bronx Bob**     Of course   my competitor is waiting outside your busted door.    Let me bring him in.    May I present **Ziggy the Zebra.**

**Ziggy Zebra**   Hello Rex and Iggy. The pleasure is all mine. Me and the boys in the **Serengeti**  loved  your show last week   or should I say competition.  It was a **spectacle,** especially the singing with the two Bob's and Carl the Coal. The **Rocket**  wow unbelievable. Tell me how are **Meco's** eyebrows? He should never have been so close to the rocket   man.

**Rex**   Meco's eyebrows are fine. The two Bobs are in Outer space and  **Serengeti,**   are we talking **Africa Tanzania** here?

**Ziggy Zebra**   Yes of course it is a magnificent place.

**Iggy**    Ziggy  maybe you could get a word to the **Magpie's  stop stealing people's jewelry**.  We found nests of jewelry everywhere after the show.

**Ziggy Zebra**     Yes those birds are very **entrepreneurial.** Now tell me are **Zonkeys** and **Zorses** real? I have never seen one before. Me and the boys were a little intrigued  like  You can do that!

**Rex**   **Yes** they are real  and yes **you can do that.**

**Ziggy Zebra**  Wow this opens up a whole new dating scene.

**Iggy**   Ziggy   why would you risk coming to **World Mastermind Headquarters**  if your life back home is so perfect?

**Ziggy Zebra**     Bronx Bob is one of my **heroes** yet is one of my fiercest competitors for my growing **empire.**   Bronx said  Hey Ziggy  let's make a deal!    He started talking and I was listening and the more I listened the more he talked and eventually he hit me with.....

**Bronx Bob**   You aren't **Zebra enough** to make this deal.

**Ziggy Zebra** Zebra enough   are you crazy I have to deal with *lions tigers* and *crocodiles* all day   Zebra enough *Pleassss!* I love a challenge and so do my boys so this was the ultimate challenge.

**Rex**   Challenge   you realize the loser gets blasted off the planet for good?

**Iggy**  Yes on the MFXY Chromosome Rocket   Like in Bye Bye you can't come back.

**Ziggy Zebra**   Yes I do realize that Bye Bye could be the outcome yet   to watch Bronx  blast off the planet into outer space   hey that would be one **happy day.**

**Bronx Bob**   Ziggy  I love your **enthusiasm** and I love your empire even more.  I don't plan on losing.   I brought a great pair of **binoculars** to watch you blast off into the great beyond.

**Ziggy Zebra**   I don't think you know who you are dealing with. Me and my boys are always **hungry** for more  but we conquer our world a little differently than you do.

**Bronx Bob**   Hungry for more   I always get what I want and  losing is not an option.

**Rex**   Wow   both of you need to take a break for a minute. How about some **cheese** and **crackers** or some **Beef jerky**?

**Ziggy Zebra**   Beef jerky don't you know that stuff is full of **sodium nitrates**

**Bronx Bob**   Yes it hardens the **arteries** as well.

**Ziggy Zebra**   Good point Bronx I hope this is not what you boys eat for a living cause your body is a **temple.**

**Bronx Bob**   Food doesn't choose you, you choose the food you eat.

**Ziggy Zebra**   It's called **lifestyle** choices and that is why **85%** of the Homo Sapiens will die of *heart disease cancer* or an *autoimmune disease.*

**Bronx Bob**   Yes as reported by the *World Health Organization* most people will never see their **81st** birthday.

**Ziggy Zebra**   Yes you Homo Sapiens are dying to long and living to short.

**Bronx Bob**   most people eat way **too** much food and never give their bodies enough **time** to **digest** the **food** they've **eaten**.

**Ziggy Zebra**   We Zebra's eat when we are hungry or when a lion eats us  whichever comes first.

**Rex  Stopppppppp!**  Wow  let's put  a hold on this riveting information for one minute   and get focused on the task at hand guys.

**Iggy**   Let's get a **clearer** picture so we **all** can be prepared for this show.

**Rex**   In the words of a famous **philosopher**

**Iggy**   the moves of a famous **concrete** dancer

**Rex**   the sound of an **unforgettable** piece of music

**Iggy**   the **taste of** a scrumptious morsel

**Rex**   and the **mask** of a famous actor in **limbo** as he is walking on a **tightrope** anguishing over his **recent** descent from **greatness** thus keeping his eye on the task at hand.....

**Rex Iggy**      Q **the Italian dance number**

> Ziggy Zebra fields of joy lifelong prosperity
> Wants to risk it all this week to rise to the challenge
> Bronx Bob wants it all the more he has the more he wants
> A bully in the playground one day he will meet his match

> Who's going to live in the rocket
> Who wants to go for a long ride
> Who wants to be this stupid
> Oh yes you both do!

> Life is a box of chocolates
> Both of you are numskulls
> Sorry to be so friggin blunt
> To risk it all this way

**Ziggy Zebra**   Wow Rex and Iggy tell me how you really feel.

**Bronx Bob**   I know you both spoke the truth no hard feelings.

**Rex**   This is a choice you're both making.

**Iggy**   We just want to make sure  as we proceed forward.

**Rex**   We have to send out our promotions and get the World ready for **Round Two.**

**Iggy**      **Bronx Bob vs Ziggy the Zebra** Winner take all **Battle Royale.**

**Bronx Bob**   Hey I love it

**Ziggy Zebra**  it's got real pizzaz

**Rex**  The competition  will it be **divided** into three sections as last week's show?

**Bronx Bob**  Yes we are **illuminating** section two and adding a new version in its place.

**Iggy**  Ok so  section one will be **introducing** yourselves to the World.

**Rex**  Section three is the **sing** and **perform** your own **song** round.

**Bronx Bob**  Yes and section two is **The potato sack obstacle course race**.

**Ziggy Zebra**  Bob and I will each have our own team of four members inside our potato sacks as we race around the course.

**Bronx Bob**  The winner will be the **first** team that gets to the finish line.

**Ziggy Zebra**  Anything goes in our attempt to win.

**Rex**  Really  this is the best you came up with? A Potato sack obstacle course race?

**Iggy**  Rex I love it. It's a **paradigm shift** in the perception of last week's show of **talk** and **music** and **adds** the third **dimension** of **strength, agility** as a new pillar.

**Rex**  Right  potato sack obstacle course race  I mean please this is what I did when I was **three** years old.

**Iggy**  This is brilliant and the audience in attendance and the viewers around the world are going to go crazy.

**Rex**  Right  We're talking potato sack obstacle course race here built for Homo Sapiens and Earth Entities on their quest for?

**Iggy**  Rex it's fabulous.  So Bronx Bob and Ziggy the Zebra let me be **absolutely** clear here  the competition is going to consist of three sections?

**Bronx Ziggy**   Yes

**Iggy**   The first round is the talking and introduction round?

**Bronx Ziggy**   Yes

**Iggy**   Round two is a potato sack obstacle course race?

**Bronx Ziggy**   Yes

**Iggy**       Round three is to write and perform your own song round?

**Bronx Ziggy**   Yes

**Iggy**       There are three judges who announce the winner after every round?

**Bronx Ziggy**   Yes

**Iggy**   After the final round the loser and his team  blast off the planet in the *MFXY Chromosome Rocket*?

**Bronx Ziggy**   Yes

**Iggy**   For good?

**Bronx Ziggy**   Yes

**Iggy**       That's what I thought you said.

**Rex**   Is everyone in agreement?

**Bronx Ziggy Iggy**   *YESSSSSSSSSS*

**Rex**   Well I think we got ourselves a real humdinger of an event

**Bronx Ziggy Iggy**   *YESSSSSSSSS*

**Iggy**   Any final words before Friday night's epic event?

**Bronx Bob Ziggy Zebra Rex Iggy**       Yesssssss **Q the sloth**

Music sloth and talking as it fades out!

# BRONX BOB

## VS

# Ziggy the Zebra

### Competition Night

**Announcer 1**   Homo Sapien Bob vs the World   Round Two
Bronx Bob vs Ziggy the Zebra in a battle of **Epicness**. Two **Multi-World** Masters of **Organizations** of     **Happy......** Is this right
Happy   Well, At this point, we're not too sure what they **actually**
do   so what kind of happiness are we talking about   yet we have
just been informed that they both  love *plants, puppy dogs,* and
*long walks* off **short piers** with **bricks** tied to the **ankles** of business **associates?** Now we're talking   *Hmmmmmm* This sounds
like it is going to be one **whale** of a night. No offense to the whales
As in the internal words of  **Lady Gaga**   Let's **Dance** with the **paparazzi** in our **poker** face  to the edge of **glory**.

**Announcer 2**   Ladies and gentleman, take your seat the show will
begin in five minutes.

**Announcer 1**     Q the studio audience
                    Q the polka band
                    Q the crying baby
                    Q the frogs
                    Q the silencing of the lambs
                    Q the rain falling on a tin roof
                    Q the Bob Dylan impersonator

**Announcer 1**     Wow, the studio audience looks energized for this epic battle   the **polka band** is really Polka king   Hey, wait a minute, is that the same **crying** baby from the last week's show? I thought we had him banned     **security**      the **frogs** croaking is attracting more croaking frogs oh noooo        the silencing of the **lambs** is kind of working         and the rain on the **hot tin roof** is raining on the   **hot wet tin roof**      and to the **Bob Dylan** impersonator   thanks, it's an honor to have you part of this show     Hey Mr. **Tambourine** man stop blown in the wind like a rolling **stone** or will send you back to Maggie's **farm** for good     Impersonator Bob enough is enough
**10 9 8 7 6 5 4 3 2 1**

**Iggy**     Wow, Rex, this is going to be one hell of a show. I thought we had a huge audience last week. This week's audience is going crazy right from the start. The **elephants** are line dancing with **banana** trees while **chickens** are pretend boxing with **corn** husks blowing in the wind, which are popping popcorn for the Homo Sapiens to eat.

*Wowwwww*     See Rex, this is the finest example of when all of Mother Earths **creations**     work together in perfect **harmony** *Rex Rex Rex   ohhhh*, I forgot you're putting on your announcer's face for the billions in attendance and watching around the world.

**Rex**   I am the master of my **domain** I am the master of my domain I am the master of my domain. Ok, I am ready, Iggy. We should practice a little   before we go on stage    we need to be entertaining right from the start.   If I say   **red**    what do you say?

**Iggy   War and Peace**

**Rex**   ohhh ok, How about   **newspaper**

**Iggy**     **Portuguese** pottery **packaging** for **procurement** of property properly.

**Rex**   Ohhhh, I think we'll be fine   *ohhhhh*   look, it's Mecoooo.

**Meco**   Hello boys, have you seen the MFXY Chromosome Rocket? It's finely tuned and waiting for the occupants for tonight's show.

**Iggy**   How could we miss it

**Meco**   It's ready for the wild blue **yonder.** Who's wild yonder Blues wild yonder   into the **sky** of forever   that's who's forever.

**Iggy**   words from a true   Rocket man

**Rex**   Wow, the Rocket looks fabulous   but do you think we can move it back a little?

**Meco**   Sure, no problem

**Rex**   In last week's show, we lost a few entities during the blast-off sequence.

**Meco**   let me contact my brother **Seco**   and get him to move it back fifty feet.

**Rex**   Wow, you have a brother   that is what I call efficiency.

**Iggy**   Meco, everyone has been wondering about your eyebrows from **last week's** show and how they fared from the blast-off?

**Rex**   you seemed to be very close to the rocket?

**Meco**   Yes, my job is **dangerous**, and  that is why I have **interchangeable** eyebrows  you can blast one pair off, and I'm ready with another.

**Rex**   I kept telling people he's the **brains** of this operation   and they'd say   why is he so close to the rocket? Does he actually know what he is doing? Brains only work when they are technically **attached** to your head.

**Meco**   I have learned to be my own **Meco** and not the **Meco** of the people who want me to be a different **Meco** than **Meco**.

**Iggy**   Did you find out why the Rocket engine didn't start last week?

**Meco**   No   rockets can be **finicky** creatures.

**Rex**   We saw you **kicking** and **banging** your **wrench** against the side of the rocket in a **semi-violent manner**   yet   with a **controlled** anger.

**Meco**   I was showing the rocket who was in charge. After the first start of the engines, it was a **no-no**   after many banging adjustments, we had a **go-go**.

**Rex**   So the rocket got the message   right

**Meco**   Yes   in the rocket business, sometimes   you have to throw **conventional** wisdom off the side of the rocket and do what **caveman** have been doing for years.

**Iggy**   Use the **tools** that the earth has **supplied** over millions of years?

**Meco**   No

**Rex**   Use the **fire** from the **sun** as the **ignition** for the **engine,** so we are **intrinsically** aligned with the **universe**?

**Meco**   No

**Iggy**   **Differentiate** yourself between **time-space vs space-time** and how we experience the world through each **dimension.**

**Meco**   No

**Rex**   Ok, what then?

**Meco**   **Prey**

**Rex**   Yes, of course, that is a great **strategy.**

**Iggy**   So let me get this straight we went from   no-no   to bang bang   to prey prey   to go go   to blast off   to bye-bye   to Bob BOB to time-space

**Meco**   Yes

**Rex**  Is there any chance of a repeat performance from the en-gines.

**Meco**  Well  if the big shiny Rocket hooked up to the **erector** gets shy and can't perform the start-up procedure  then we might have to take drastic **measures** with the **thrusters** and bend them that might get messy.

**Iggy**  No one wants their thrusters bent.

**Rex**  Wow, let's hope it never gets to that point.

**Iggy**  Do you have any special message for everyone for this show?

**Meco Iggy Rex Iggy**     Q The Music

### I'm Meco I'm Rocket man

Blastoff from the erector
MFXY Chromosome Rocket
I got big bad shiny shiny rocket
moving parts that need to be adjusted

Little puffs of smoke   Coming out the sides
Hey there's no smoking   If you wanna die

I'm Meco I'm rocket man
I'm brains bloody operation
Got wrenches, welder torches, brushes tools, and sprockets
Look after my shiny shiny rocket

Wise man say
Screw the wise man this bad boy has got to get up in the air
Blow his top like it's going to pop
Explode for the ages time for lift-off

I'm Meco I'm Rocket man
I've got eyebrows another week another pair
I'm Meco I'm Rocket man

I've got brains E- Pluribus Unum to the 1
I'm Meco I'm Rocket man
I've got tools anything you want adjusted
I'm Meco I'm Rocket man
Start your engines Blast-off into the sky

**Announcer 1**   Ladies and gentlemen, please take your seats the show is about to begin.

**Rex**   Wow  Iggy  look, Bronx Bob is talking with Ziggy the Zebra before the big show I wonder what they're saying?

**Iggy**    **Hey**  this sounded like a great idea at the beginning of the week?   *hahaha*

**Rex**    Knowing Bronx Bob, he's establishing territory control for his certain win    or giving Ziggy some sloth lessons, *hahaha.*

**Iggy**    We will find out soon enough    *ohhh,* look who it is,  Rex.

**Rex**    **Mother Earth**, I'm so glad you made tonight's show and are one of the **judges.** We need your **leadership** and **stewardship** as a symbol of **hope** to all the Entities and Homo Sapiens out there that call Earth home. This is a very **delicate** time in the **history** of our **planet.**

**Mother Earth**   Rex, have you **tried** the **shrimp** rings? They are to **die** for   no offense to the shrimp out there, yet they are tastier than **caviar**, no offense to the **sturgeon.**

**Iggy**    Mother Earth, as we balance the planet back to pre Homo Sapien status, how long will it take before we see the fruits of our labor through these competitions start to take hold?

**Mother Earth**    Iggy, can you please be a dear and take hold of my dish of **crab legs** as I'm trying to **reach** for another **Pina Colada** in a **coconut** mug.

**Rex**    Mother Earth, is there a  message you would like to convey to the rest of the planet.

**Mother Earth**   Rex and Iggy I'm a gal that has seen many **moons** over my billions of years from **Super** Moons **micro** moons **harvest** moons, **red** moons, **blood** moons, and many many **more** moons, yet the moon I recall most of all   was when I met   **Keith's Moon.**

**Rex Iggy  WHO**

**Mother Earth**   Keith's Moon   wow   he could **pound** his **drums** all over my **generation**  as my **face** dances with delight   like a **savage** who are you?   I would scream, **beast**    let me remind you, still keeping his **rhythm** announcing to whoever was listening   **who's next**.   It's **hard** were his words of **wisdom**     seeing I was the only one there I found his words *humorous, engaging, spiritual,* and pounding like an **aphrodisiac**.   I will never forget Keith's Moon, **if you know what I mean.**

**Rex**   Ok   not really      *ohhhh* look   it's **Father Time**   thank god, just in the nick of time.

**Iggy**    Father Time, how do you feel about Bronx Bob being part of the competition this week?

**Father Time**    I ain't got time for this crap.

**Iggy**    Ok   How about Mother Earth's version of the **celestial expressions** of the various moons from the book of moon's and Keith's Moon.

**Father Time**   Who   I ain't got time for this crap if you know what I mean.

**Rex**   I love how Father Time is so **direct** with his subtle clues of wisdom mixed in with **sarcasm** slash rationale **panache** for the moment.

**Iggy**   Yes, he truly is one of earth's treasures of knowledge   he does so much with so little, **if you know what I mean.**   Hey, I have our third judge in front of me right now, **Mother Nature.** You are looking **radiant** as ever. How do you see tonight's competition folding out?

**Mother Nature**   Yes, Iggy  don't get me started on radiant   my light is a **beacon**   and on Sunday, it's all about a beacon for **bacon** and tonight's competition   all I know is that Zebra better bring his **A game** cause Bronx Bob has got some **fast** hands **if you know what you mean.**

**Rex**   Honestly   I don't know what anyone means anymore? Mother Nature as the **third** judge, do you see the balance of **power** starting to shift if the Homo Sapiens lose tonight's competition sending the Earth Entities on to a second straight **victory,** or are we too soon into these competitions to see any difference?

**Mother Nature** What?

**Iggy**   What Rex is trying to say in Mother Nature's words is   The **Wind** blows the **tree** over with a **thud,** and the tree stays on the ground **sleeping**   it becomes a nursery **log** with **moss** slowly starting to **decay** to feed the ground below   and above. This second win could put the Homo Sapiens on the ground for good yet in the sky for bye-bye.

**Mother Nature**   You boys  got some serious problems. If we are talking about the **quantum** world again, you better get your facts straight. Now excuse me while I get my toenails cut before the start of this show.

**Rex**   Well, she seems a little **temperamental t**onight.

**Iggy**   I keep forgetting she has the four seasons to deal with. I hope that doesn't cloud her judgment on tonight's show.

**Rex**  Iggy, it looks like we are moments away from the start of the show. How do you feel? Do you have any last-minute questions, words of encouragement, or advice before we throw ourselves in front of billions around the world?

**Iggy**   Hey  I feel great, Rex no nerves, pretty relaxed I think this show has all the ear **markings** of a classic show.

**Rex** When you say ear markings are we talking left or right **hoop's posts** or **manholes** of space inside the **eardrum** you can toss peas through or the **continuum** of mark and his kings.

**Iggy** It would depend if we are talking pre sixteenth century or not.

**Announcer 1** Ladies and Gentlemen, please make your way to your seats.

The show is about to begin
And now a message from our sponsor

**Announcer 2** Tonight's show is sponsored by **Mac Row** and **Saul**, your expert window cleaners. Start me up with that Mac Row Saul windows start me up with that Mac Row Saul windows start me up start me up start me upppppppp.

**Announcer 1** We hope you enjoy the show
Ladies and Gentlemen, your host for tonight's event

**Announcer 2** Rex and Iggy

**Rex** Good Evening Home Sapiens and Earth Entities from around the world I'm Rex, your announcer with my sidekick Iggy. We welcome you to **Homo Sapien Bob vs The World.** Tonight's competition consists of two captains of their industries **Bronx Bob** and **Ziggy the Zebra**.

**Iggy** Hello everyone, I'm Iggy. A special shout out to all the **babysitters** that can't make tonight's show because they are sitting with **babies**. To the babies who are watching the babysitters **sitting** watching them you baby's rock with your baby sitters!

**Rex** Now, under the rules of the governing body of announcers worldwide and to the **Amendment** of article **19.7** in the third sessions of the only **Fairness Act** and a few other acts of acting, it just means WFU approved.

**Iggy**  Lets raise the curtain for tonight's **Epic battle.**

**Rex**  In the **black** and **gold** corner, we've got Bronx Bob, who weighs in at **200** lbs. say hi, Bronx Bob.

**Bronx Bob**  Hi Bronx Bob

**Iggy**  In the **white** and **black striped** corner, we've got Ziggy the Zebra, who weighs in at **800** lbs. say hi Ziggy the Zebra.

**Ziggy Zebra**  Hi Ziggy The Zebra man

**Rex**  Both competitors look raring to go on their quest for world domination   as they like to call it    were not sure what world domination means    yet   they both have the **eye** of the tiger.

**Iggy**  Ziggy actually brought a **real** eye of a tiger   wow    this is going to be great   Bronx doesn't look fazed.

**Rex**  Let's get this competition underway, and in **round one**, it's

**Rex and Iggy**   *Meet and Greet*

**Iggy**  Each competitor has 3 minutes to introduce themselves to the world.

**Rex**  Our first competitor **Bronx Bob** the Homo Sapien, has agreed to go first now, Bronx Bob, if you're ready   Let's Get It On......

**Bronx Bob**  Hello, my name is Bronx Bob, and I was born and raised in **New York City** let me be a little more specific The Bronx. The school of **hard Knocks** is what I like to call it. This is where I sharpened my skills as a young savvy, let's say, entrepreneur. Other kids had paper routes, rode their **bicycles,** and played **baseball**. I, on the other hand, had a team of **drivers** on routes everywhere in **New York** delivering, let's call it **stuff.**

Then I got a great idea one day. I started to hire the *paper route gang* as I liked to call them for some of my other routes and **10X** what they made delivering papers eventually, no one got newspapers. The parents of these kids became some of my best customers as I expanded into more and more areas. Eventually, I bought the daily **newspaper** and got rid of the paper and kept the customers. A stroke of genius, these people loved what I supplied them.

My parents always challenged me to be greater, so they kicked me out of the house at fifteen. They told me to come back when I became *respectable, responsible,* and *resourceful.* I thought I was all of those and more?

In my parents' eyes, they saw the potential yet had a hard time expressing **gratitude** when I bought them a new home at the age of sixteen with cash. They couldn't understand why I didn't buy them the house next to my Dad's brother's kids house two streets over.

So I became **obsessed** with business and bought some new knuckles because I liked the way they **shone** in the moonlight, which doubled my business and territory overnight. Funny how that happened. My parents kept reminding me about the *Three R's* and the house I didn't buy them.

Marriage was not one of my **strong points**, and I was only dragged down the aisle once. My line of work usually puts a bit of stress on the Misses. The constant late **nights, partying, clothing, friends, psychiatrists, trips, money**, I don't know how I put up with her nonsense over the years.

Our relationship was strictly a **one-way** affair. Imagine a **road**, a **driver,** a **car**, some **gas**   yet   you don't know where you are going so you only drive straight   realizing you haven't even turned on the **damn** car.

If that doesn't turn your crank or make sense, say you had a **cow** with many **utters**, and they all needed to be working and producing milk at the same time. One utter gets **dislodged** and starts firing the milk in the opposite direction. You would start questioning whether that utter might not be **aligned** with the other utters.

If that doesn't make sense, too bad, get on with it!

One day I found my **wife** with my cousin **Rocco**. Apparently, he was inspecting one of my wife's **utters** in the car parked in the garage. Today we have a very **amicable** relationship. I have no idea where **she** is and Rocco, well last time I saw him he was heaped over in a **pool** of..... Funny, I haven't seen him either.

Me and the Misses did have an offspring, little **Bobbi Bronx**. He's following in his Dad's footprints. He has a **real** paper route, practices **Tai chi**, and **volunteers** at the **soup** kitchens, so he lives at his **grandparents'** house.

My business adventures are spread throughout North, Central, and South America and into the European Union. I am what you call the **Business Aficionado** if I see a great business I like and I can dominate, then I get to know that business really fast. It is about the timing and the bottom line.

My business acronym is **BB3R**, which stands for *Bronx Bob 3 R's.* All of my business associates have this tattooed on their butts. We *restructure* new businesses to fit in with our business philosophy, we *rehabilitate* the nonbelievers to believers, and finally, we get *results*. If we don't see the results, we do more rehabilitating, if you know what I mean. Everyone learns to love the BB3R formula.

Today I am on the lookout for **sustainable** growth businesses you know that are more in alignment with the planet. They need to grow from the ground up and are great for **distribution.** You can groom for a new generation, which leads to **gargantuan gains**. I call these **addictive** assets of growth for the *Twenty-First Century.*

The Bronx Bob organization of **hundreds** of companies wants to work with Mother Earth, Father Time, and Mother Nature to help balance the planet back to respectability, responsibility, and re-sourcefulness and also so we can restructure, rehabilitate and get results.

Thanks, Bronx Bob

**Rex**  Thanks, Bronx Bob that was a deep dive into the world of the Bronx, very inspirational and

**Iggy**  Yes, maybe a little **brownie** points added in at the end for some good measure great  Job  Bronx Bob  I'm sure the judges loved it.

**Rex**  Yes, now for our next competitor **Ziggy the Zebra**, who comes from the plains of the Serengeti in Tanzania, Africa.

**Iggy**  Ziggy, if you are ready for the challenge, Bronx Bob put on a great opening round **soliloquy**  so in the words of Barry White let's get it on....

**Ziggy Zebra**  Hi everyone. I'm Ziggy the Zebra. I'm 800 hundred pounds of Zebra **joy** wrapped in **black and white** stripes here to tell you about my life on the plains of the **Serengeti** from **yesterday** and **today**. It is literally two different worlds within one world.

I was born in **East Africa** while on route traveling across **Tanzania** and **Kenya** in what is called the **Great Migration**. Hundreds of thousands of *Wildebeest Zebras* and *Antelope* make the trek across the plains each year in search of a better place to **graze** safer areas to **breed** and give **birth** to more zebras. Hey, a world with more zebra's is a good world, look at us, we're adorable.

My parents found each other in a sea of Zebras in The Great Migration one year. Have you ever seen what thousands of Zebras look like? Now picture thousands and thousands of Zigging and Zagging Zebras all moving with rotating **ears** listening for predators **snorting** and **barking** signals with wide-open **eyes** and **teeth** shining. We is what beautiful is.

You might also be thinking, how do Zebras find each other when we all **look** and **sound** the same? Each one of us has a **unique** and different striped pattern, and no **two** patterns are the same. This is similar to a Homo Sapien, which uses a **fingerprint** for **identification.** Stripes fingerprints I mean please, man, it's obvious which one is better, don't you think?

My parents said it was love at first sight and stripe when they met. The courting didn't last long because **thirteen** months later, Ziggy, the Zebra man, was born. Once I dropped, I haven't stopped moving. I'm like the energizer *bunny*, yet I am a proud zebra man, **less** the bunny.

I went on many migrations with my parents throughout the years and traveled vast areas of land, each **trek** being a little different. We zebras and the other animals would come together for a collective to protect ourselves from the *lions, tigers,* and *crocodiles.*

Why they would want to eat us is beyond me. We're too beautiful to eat. We are like the **Picasso** of the animal world. No one wants to eat a Picasso. Maybe a **pistachio** but never a Picasso.

My parents had a mutual bond for **curiosity,** which led them down the rabbit hole of Zebra **Lore.** While most Zebras followed the **code** of conduct, my parents were off discovering new lands, adventures and studying the Zebra habitat. They were true pioneers, and I was a quick study.

Their groundbreaking work proved that Zebras actually had black coats with white stripes while one color attracted the sun, the other repelled the sun. They also discovered that the stripe pattern acted as a **camouflage** of distance to other animals and as a form of pest control.

We Zebra's assumed we had white coats with black stripes. We were still being taken out for lunch by lions, **yet** not as often as the other animals. **Insects** had a hard time figuring out where to land because of our stripes, so they flew and bit the other animals.

They were ahead of their time   kind of like **Einstein** was   yet in the Zebra world.

I miss my parents   they are why I am able to do the work I do today. They eventually **succumbed** to their **curiosity** when they **drifted** too far from the other Zebra's and could not make it back. They were an **inspiration** to the rest of the Zebra's. I decided to carry on their **groundbreaking** work yet in a little different way.

I don't do the migration thing anymore. I do what is called *cross-pollination* with *germination* with a whole lot of *irrigation* with worldwide distribution. I develop greener pastures after the other Zebras have left for a better place to graze.

You could say we are like **caretakers** for the land. We redevelop older areas along with new areas to strengthen the **ecosystem** so Mother Earth and Mother Nature can do their thing. Father Time, I haven't figured out what he does, yet he might allow us the time to follow through with our mission.

We teach other entities the skills they need to be resourceful as well. We all work together through our organization and distribution channels, so It is a *win-win* situation for everyone.

I have a network of zebras who are my **associates,** and our goal is a healthy planet for everyone. It just so happens our plant of choice is loved by millions. We have developed many products and are constantly **expanding**. Our business partners are everywhere, and we can't supply them with enough product.

Who are our customers? **Homo Sapiens**. Apparently, they have found many uses for our products, and **governments** around the world are relaxing the laws, so we seem to be in the sweet spot of commerce.

What started out with missing a migration has led me on this journey into a new world. I think my parents would be proud of me as I am following in their footprints. Thanks, Ziggy the Zebra man.

**Rex** Wow Ziggy, the Zebra man, brought it that was **electric** who knew he was such a **gardener** for the planet. Bronx Bob has got to be worried I don't know if he brought enough to win this round from Ziggy.

**Iggy** Yes, that was absolutely fabulous, and I know the judges were taking notes and eating food. Each competitor's opening remarks were strong on what they brought to the planet.

**Rex** Iggy, let's face it, the judges have a huge decision to make this round could go either way.

**Iggy** Yes, Rex, no *pressure cooker* here

**Rex** Mother Earth, Mother Nature, and Father Time, as we like to call them the **triple-decker** I think, are ready now to give us their winners for this first round.

**Iggy** Yes, each judge, has a name on a big card which they will reveal to the world. It looks like Mother Earth will be first to show us her card Wow **Ziggy The Zebra**

**Rex** Father time looks like he's next, and his card reads **Bronx Bob.**

**Iggy** That means whatever is on Mother Nature's card will indicate the winner of round one **DRummmmm Rolllll.**

**Rex** and the winner of round one is **Ziggy the Zebra.**

**Iggy** Wow, the crowd is going wild and Bronx Bob looks visibly upset. He wants to **challenge** the voting system already.

**Rex** Remember he is a man that usually gets what he wants and hates to lose.

**Announcer 2** Round two will be happening in a few minutes we are just setting up the **potato sack obstacle course race.** There will be no contesting the results from round one. Ladies and gentlemen, **streeeetch** we will be with you shortly.

**Rex**   Wow, Iggy, that was a remarkable first round, and it looks like we have Ziggy the Zebra here to comment on his first-round win. Ziggy, you are the real gardener for the earth how do you feel about this first-round win.

**Ziggy Zebra**   Hey, I believe in myself. I give what the earth supplies to me to make this planet a better place to live. It just so happens I can **earn** a little, let me rephrase that, **alot** of **dough** in the process. Also, I teach my skills to other Entities to grow our presence on the earth.

**Iggy**   Wow, thanks, Ziggy the Zebra now we have Bronx Bob here. Bronx Bob tell us how you felt about the results for that first round.

**Bronx Bob**   Iggy, I don't believe the judges even heard my message. Father Time is the only one who **articulated** what I had to say. I think the other two were busy **eating** and got distracted from the message about the earth. I'm all **earth man** in fact, I should be called **Bronx Bob Earth Man.**

**Iggy**   Thanks Bronx Bob Earth Man

**Rex**   Wow, Iggy, that was really **intense**, yet I believe Ziggy the Zebra was the clear winner his message was spot on.

**Iggy**   Yes, I have to agree with you. Now **Round two** is the potato sack obstacle course race. Each team will have four team members **maneuvering** their way around the course inside their own potato sack.

**Rex**   There will be three obstacle **challenge** points along the way, which are meant to **challenge** each team. Like **duhhhh**

**Iggy**   The Zebra team will have a total of **sixteen** legs inside each sack, and trying to coordinate should be a tough one. Bronx Bob's team will only have **eight** legs to deal with.

**Rex**   If I was a betting man, I think Bronx Bob will have the edge with less legs involved.

**Iggy**   Let me remind you   Bronx Bob has got to win this round because if he loses, he will be the next Bob to blast off.

**Iggy**   I think this is where we are going to see Bronx Bob at his best. There is no way he is going to let this **slip** through his fingers and end up in outer space on a rocket.

**Announcer 2**   Ladies and Gentleman Round Two The Potato Sack Obstacle Course Race.

**Rex**   Each team will have to climb into their own one big potato sack and maneuver themselves around the course. The judges will be looking for **infractions** along the way.

**Iggy**   Yes, the only infraction I see right now is **ear-biting**, thanks to **Mike Tyson** on that one.

**Rex**   Well, here we go, the teams are at the starting gate Bronx and his team looks **unstoppable**, and Ziggy's team looks relaxed like hey, it's just another day at the **Rodeo**.

### Bang

**Rex**   There off and running and believe it   Ziggy's team has got off to a **blazing** start they are in a full gallop   they look like poetry in motion. **Sixteen** zebra legs tucked inside that sack, all zigging and zagging along what a sight. Their lead is now stretching to thirty feet.

**Iggy**   Bronx Bob's team looks a little out of rhythm. They have yet to find their **stride**, yet Bronx has got that **hell-bent** for anything goes face on. If anyone will figure this out, it will be Bronx he doesn't lose and especially two times in one night, that's unheard of.

**Iggy**   Looks like Ziggy and his team are coming up to the first obstacle. This obstacle is called **The Full Meal Deal.** Each team must exit their potato sack and sit down to eat a *hamburger, large* *fries,* and a *coke.*

**Rex**    Yes, very peculiar the Zebras, are **protesting** as they sit down to their Full Meal Deal challenge    their **vegetarians** and they don't eat meat. This could be a **game-changer.** Did they not read the rules before the race started?

**Iggy**    Wow, Bronx Bob and his team have just arrived and have jumped out of their potato sack and are running to the table. They have **meat-eaters** written all over their bodies. They are **devouring** the burgers, fries, and a cokes like the hungry carnivores they are.

**Rex**    Yes Bronx and his team looks **unstoppable** as the zebras are still trying to figure out how to eat the hamburger. It seems like one Zebra is taking the plunge and just swallowed one hamburger whole. Now the other zebras are **tossing** the rest of the hamburgers and fries into his mouth as he looks like he is going to gag.

**Iggy**    What a scene the Bronx team is just finishing up their meals and have jumped into their potato sack and have gotten out into an early lead. Ziggy and his team are now carrying their *wounded warrior meat eater* to the potato sack where he looks green. Yes, the judges are over, making sure the zebras ate all the burgers fries and cokes.

**Rex**    Wow, this is fabulous. Bronx Bob is now stretching his lead as the four-man team has now got that **Bob rhythm** going strong. They have a slow climb up this ramp where their next obstacle awaits them. Ziggy's team is now running with three zebras as the meat-eater collapses in the potato sack as they are having to **drag** him along.

**Iggy**    Bronx Bob and his team have now arrived at the second obstacle. It looks like it is a **giant map** of the world in **Jigsaw form**. It looks like they have to put the pieces together to form the World before they can move on.

**Rex**    This should be easy for both teams seeing they both have businesses that are global.

**Iggy**   What is it they do again?

**Rex**   I have no idea. Ziggy and his team have just arrived and have placed their wounded meat-eater zebra off to the side so the other three can concentrate on the World map.

**Iggy**   The meat-eater Zebra now looks like he is turning a lighter shade of **pale** as he is **skipping** in the light of the **fandango.**

**Rex**   Fandango, I think he's doing **cartwheels** to see if he can dislodge the meat. No, I think he is feeling sick *lookout........*

**Iggy**   Yes, the crowd is going **wild** and calling out for more! Wow, this is action. Bronx Bob's team has the America's portion assembled and is now working on the other half of the world.

**Rex**   Ziggy's team has assembled  Africa and European Union in lightning-fast fashion and now is starting to put the America's together.

**Iggy**   Frustrations are mounting from both teams as they are looking at each other's maps to **distinguish** where the different parts of the world go. Bronx Bob's team looks like they are almost finished, yet I think they have the North and south poles mixed up.

**Rex**   You are right the judges just pointed that out, and Ziggy's team is now stuck with North America and South America. The crowd is at a fever pitch, screaming out to each team.

**Iggy**   Bronx Bob's team has finished the assembly of the world. The judges have given the **thumbs-up** sign, and they are off to the potato sack for the last obstacle in this epic race.

**Rex**   Ziggy, the Zebra man, has just lost his cool no hold on he has a **popsicle** in his mouth, my bad. They finally figured out where **Florida** went, and the **judges** have given the **thumbs-up** sign, and now the Zebras are off to the potato sack and on to the course.

**Iggy**  At this point, Rex  Bronx Bob has a **huge lead**  over Ziggy The Zebra's team, yet there is still **one** more obstacle to go.  Then there will be that  final dash to the finish line. It looks like the meat-eating Zebra is back and is maybe **49 shades of grey** now.

**Rex**  That is a **vast** improvement over what we saw a short time ago. The Zebra **mojo** we saw at the beginning looks like it is back.

**Iggy**  You betcha Rex they are starting to gain some ground on Bronx Bob's team.

**Rex**  Looks Like Bronx Bob's team is heading into the **third** obstacle. Wow, you're not going to believe this it's a version of **pin the tail** on the **donkey** with *live Donkeys.*

**Iggy**  Those poor donkeys they never seem to get a break. Ziggy's team has just arrived and has jumped out of their potato sack full of confidence.

**Rex**  Hey, you know what Iggy  Zebras **look** more like Donkeys than Bronx Bob's team does.

**Iggy**  Good one Rex that was a brilliant observation.

**Rex**  Now, the **object** of this obstacle is to place the tail on the *live donkey* within a certain **radius** of where the tail goes. Each competitor is **blindfolded** and **spun** around **three** times before they get to put the tail on the *live donkey.* Whichever team places the tail with the sharp end into the tail region of the *live donkey*  can then proceed to **dash** to the **finish line**.

**Iggy**  One last note the *live donkey* will let out a **yelp** when that region of tail area is reached,  those poor donkeys haven't we done enough to damage their **demeanor**.

**Rex**  Yes, the more these teams miss, the meaner those **live donkeys** are going to get.

**Iggy**  Were just making an **ass** out of them at this point.

**Rex**    Bronx Bob is now being blindfolded and spun and is now heading towards the *live donkey* and        *Ohhhhh*, he pinned the tail on the *live donkey's* **nose**. The *live Donkey* **grimaces**, and Bronx Bob has some **foul** words for the grimacing one.

**Iggy**    It wasnt the *live donkeys* fault.

**Rex**    Bronx Bob wasn't happy for what ever reason.

**Iggy**    Again Rex  those poor Donkeys, now they have to put up with personal insults.

**Rex**    Get over it, Iggy  the donkeys have had a **bum rap** for years, yet this could be their **finest** moment. Ziggy the Zebra is getting blindfolded and turned around and is heading towards the *Live donkey* and look out  *ohhhhhh* He just gave his Donkey an **earring**.

**Iggy**    This looks harder than it seems. Next up is one of Bronx Bob's boys  he is now being blindfolded and spun and is heading towards their *live donkey*, and *ooohhhhh*   that's got to hurt    so close as the *live donkey* grimaces in pain.  He has attached the tail to the *live donkeys*...... can we say **penis.**

**Rex**    No Iggy, this is a family show  try **Johnston**  instead.

**Iggy**    Yes, the *live donkeys Johnston has a tail.* Wow, so close yet so far.

**Rex**    Bronx Bob's *live Donkey* doesn't look too happy with a tail hanging from his     *Johnston.*

**Iggy**    Next up is Ziggy's team member, the meat-eater Zebra. They have blindfolded him and are now spinning him around.

**Rex**    If I was a betting man, Iggy  this is not a very good decision because........

**Iggy**    *Ohhhhhh     myyyyyyy*    the meat-eating Zebra is now throwing up hamburgers  he must have swallowed most of them **whole**  doesn't he know he should have **chewed** them first?

**Rex**     Well, the meat-eater Zebra, is turning **green** with white stripes with a black jacket. He is now **staggering** towards the donkey, blindfolded like a *drunken sailor*, and misses the donkey all together and falls to the ground in a **heap** of unchewed French fries.

**Iggy**   Don't these Zebra's realize they have to **chew** their food?

**Rex**     This could cost them this round and potentially getting blasted off the planet.

**Iggy**   The next Bronx Bob team member is now heading towards their *Live donkey,* and a team member from Ziggy the Zebras team is making his way towards his *live donkey* and     **Heehaw Heehaw**     wow **simultaneously** both teams have pinned the tail on their *live donkeys*, and now a **battle royal** between both teams has broken out.

**Rex**     Each team is preventing the other team from getting to their potato sacks for the dash to the finish line.

**Iggy**   I can see the finish line from here, yet both teams are in **full metal pedal** royale battle *extraordinaire.*

**Rex**     The rules state that at least **one** team member has to make it across the **finish** line to win this portion of the race. Who would have thought you would see Zebras and Bob's fighting like this.

**Iggy**   This is an epic battle. Bronx Bob is taking out Zebras, with one **shot** at a time. There seems to be only one Zebra left, which just so happens to be Ziggy.

**Rex**     Ziggy has two of Bob's team members in a **headlock** with his legs.

**Iggy**   The other Bob he has head-butted they are all screaming *uncle uncle uncle.*

**Rex**     Yes, it is now down to Bronx Bob and Ziggy the Zebra as Bronx Bob has decided to **stop** fighting and jumps into his potato sack and **throws** Ziggy's sack off to the side.

**Iggy**  At this point, Bob looks like he is on his way to victory as Ziggy's potato sack is too far away to **retrieve** it, so he does what zebras do best: he **chases** after Bronx Bob in his potato sack.

**Rex**  What a scene as Bronx Bob is getting closer to the finish line. Ziggy is now **gaining** ground on him and has now **leaps** into the potato sack along with Bronx Bob.

**Iggy**    *Ohhhhh,* this is unbelievable Bronx Bob and Ziggy the Zebra are now **rolling** down the hill in one potato sack towards the finish line.

**Rex**   this is going to be so close   oh my **goodness,** they cross the finish line as the **cameras** go off I have no idea who the winner is.

**Iggy**  This is definitely going to be a **photo finish.** Rex what a battle down the stretch.

**Rex**   Yes, Iggy, it lived up to its billing as a battle royale. It looks like the Triple Decker Mother Earth, Mother Nature, and Father time are now reviewing the **photographs** at the finish line to see who's head was first.

**Iggy**  Bronx Bob has definitely got a **big** head.

**Rex**   Yet Ziggy the Zebra has a **big** nose, so it could come down to who's head or nose is **bigger.**

**Iggy**  Let me remind everyone in the studio audience and around the world that if Bronx Bob loses    he will end up on planet Bob somewhere in the **milky way** courtesy of the MFXY Chromosome Rocket.

**Rex**  *Planet Bronx Bob,* let's not get ahead of ourselves.

**Iggy**  It looks like Mother Earth is about to announce the winner.

**Mother Earth**    Let's give Bronx Bob and Ziggy the Zebra a big hand what a battle, yet we can only have one winner. Can anyone say **Photo** finish? Now before I announce the winner of this second round could someone be a dear and get me some **poutine.** The French fries with **gravy** and **cheese** are almost the perfect food **combo** after a big race like this. I was getting tired watching you **combatants** battle it out, so I must eat. It was like the time I was watching **King Arthur** at **Camelot** hold court at the famous **round** table with all his **knights**. The table was more *oblong-shaped* than round. I tried to point this out to Arthur, yet I think he was **color** blind, and when he traced out the table to be built, it was dark outside. The poor **craftsmen** assigned to build the oblong table were **punished** and ended up carrying donkeys on their backs.

**Bronx Bob   Mother Earth**  will you, please announce the winner.

**Mother Earth**   ohh yea, I forgot  **Bronx Bob**   by an **ear lobe**.

**Rex**   Wow, an earlobe of Bronx Bob, was the difference there are no words to describe the *pandemonium* that has erupted around the studio audience.

**Iggy**   Yes, *bedlam* of epic *proportions*. We just received a ruling on the last part of the race stating that both contestants were **disqualified** because they broke the rules.

**Rex**   Yes when Bronx Bob threw Ziggy's potato sack off to the side, and Ziggy was running without his potato sack?

**Iggy**   Both disqualifications were **offset** from each other, and Bronx's earlobe was the difference and has now been announced as the winner of **round two.**

**Announcer 2**   Ladies and gentlemen, please take your seats. The next round will begin in a few minutes.

**Iggy**   Rex, my pulse is still racing. I have no words to describe what I just witnessed.

**Rex**   I think this will go down in history as    where were you when **X**  happened  type of moments.

**Iggy**   Your right Rex    like where were you when man *landed* on the *moon* with one giant *step*

**Rex**   Or when the *Berlin* wall came tumbling *down* to the ground

**Iggy**    or when we witnessed the *OJ Simpson* chase in the *Bronco* televised around the world

**Rex**   Lets throw in *Woodstock* and *Jimmy Hendrix.*

**Iggy**    *Yesssss*    also when you heard the *Bay City Rollers* for the first time and couldn't believe they were the next *Beatles.*

**Rex Iggy   SATURDAY NIGHT**    please

**Iggy**    yes yes Yes all fine moments in history, yet the final scene of Bronx Bob and Ziggy the Zebra rolling and heading for the finish line is a sight that will live in **infamy.**

**Rex**   Now, our next round will be the *write, sing* and *perform* your own song round.

**Iggy**   Each competitor will have to incorporate **elements** of why they **belong** here on planet Earth to **impress** our judges.

**Rex**   Yes, and if their song does not **convey** the message in a **clear** and **concise** way, they will be heading into the wild blue yonder.

**Iggy**   As so **eloquently** expressed by our Rocket man Meco. This should be a wild affair as what surprises **lurk** in the background.

**Rex**   Who thought Bob from last week's show singing *Bob spelled backward is Bob*    would be accompanied by the international superstar BoooB.

**Iggy**   And they lost to Carl the Coal, who was the **real deal.** Carl was a force of nature with his performance.

**Rex**   Carl was outstanding, so who knows what will happen tonight. The winner of this **final round** will be staying on Planet Earth to continue with their life and the loser.

**Iggy**    Well, let's just say outer space is going to get a little bit more crowded up there.

**Rex**    Here we go it looks like Bronx Bob is almost ready for his song.

**Iggy**    He has that look of **hey**    no one is going to stop me.

**Rex**    Ladies and Gentlemen, this is the final round, and Bronx Bob will be performing his song first, so if we are ready, Bronx Bob, the stage is all yours.

**Bronx Bob singing**

### The Business Aficionado

New York City The school of the hard knocks
Where I honed my skill people do what I want
I'm obsessed with the Do Ra Me I follow the money
Don't give me your poor excuse I only want results

Resurrection simple truth I want what I see
Rehabilitation simple truth better work it out
You better tow the line you better get on board
You better understand I always get what I want

I'm Bronx Bob the Business Aficionado
I'm Bronx Bob the Business Aficionado
I'm Bronx Bob the Business Aficionado
I'm Bronx Bob the Business Aficionado

North Central South America The European Union to
Tentacles reach far and why I'm never satisfied
What you got I want There's room to grow
I only want what's best we can work it out

I'm your global Ambassador heavy heart with a heavy hand
Mother Earth Nature, and Time who unites like I can
One world is what I see no need to confuse the masses
Bronx Bob at the wheel we're going to get what we want

I'm Bronx Bob the Business Aficionado
I'm Bronx Bob the Business Aficionado
I'm Bronx Bob the Business Aficionado
I'm Bronx Bob the Business Aficionado
I'm Bronx Bob the Business Aficionado
I'm Bronx Bob the Business Aficionado
I'm Bronx Bob the Business Aficionado
I'm Bronx Bob I get what I want

**Rex**   What a solid offering from Bronx Bob it had all the elements of what we **love** and **hate** about **egomaniacs**. Bronx Bob is one confident **dude** and seems to have that **me** against the **world** attitude.

**Iggy**   Now Rex, he is a man of **passion**, and that was felt in his whole song. He knows what he wants. I just don't know if he spelled out **enough** of why he should **stay** on the **planet** to continue his efforts for the good of the earth.

**Rex**   The judges will have a huge job ahead of them to figure this one out. Next up is our **friendly** four-legged Ziggy the Zebra Man. I have a feeling he is going to be a strong contestant.

**Iggy**   He looks relaxed and confident and has a huge smile on his face. He is ready for his performance.

**Rex**   Ladies and Gentlemen, without further **ado**, may I present Ziggy the Zebra.

### Ziggy Zebra Sings
#### Build a Better World

Hey I'm Ziggy Zebra Wrapped in Black and White stripes
Hey I'm Ziggy Zebra I'm the pride of the Serengeti

I was born and raised in East Africa
In what is called The Great Migration
Traveling across Kenya to Tanzania
Searching for a better place to graze and give birth

My parents taught me to be curious
My parents taught me to be resourceful
All the time be the change you want to see
Open eyes we all can see so I believe

Hey I'm Ziggy Zebra I wanna change the world to a happier place
Hey Mr. Lion get off of my ass let me show you a better
Way we live in peace and harmony
No need to fight no more
Build a better world for us to grow grow grow grow

I am what you call the great caretaker
We work the lands to take care of us
We grow the crop everybody loves
Hey Big Brother about time you wake up wake up

Mother Earth a planet for everyone
Live and Breathe a world for anyone
All the time be the change you want to see
Open eyes we all can see so I believe

Hey I'm Ziggy Zebra I want to change the world to a happier place
Hey Mr. Tiger get off my ass let me show you a better
Hey I'm Ziggy Zebra I want to change the world to a happier place
Hey Mr. Crocodile get off my ass let me show you a better

Way we live in peace and harmony
No need to fight no more
Build a better world for us build a better world for us
Build a better world for us to grow grow grow grow

**Rex**   *Ohhhhhhh* my goodness   **The Zebra Man** wants a **better** world   a **happier** place   somewhere no one can **bite** his **ass** what a **fabulous** performance from the **stripped** one.

**Iggy**   Yes, a **monster** performance from  The Ziggy Man  he **blew** the **house** down   he blew the house down.   How would you like to be a judge for this one?

**Rex**   And to think the loser will be in outer space on the MFXY Chromosome Rocket in a **few minutes** is hard to comprehend. Both Bronx and Ziggy **brought** it   big time.

**Iggy**   You are right, Rex  they both sang **their** hearts out   and the judges have a **real** hard decision to make.

**Rex**   The judges look like they're getting ready to announce a winner. As in the first round, each judge will hold up a card with who they deemed as the winner.

**Iggy**   At this point, I have no idea it should be a toss em.

**Rex**   Looks like we are ready to announce the winner.

**Iggy**   Yes, Mother Earth is going to be first   she is now coming to the front of the stage and turns over her card  **Ziggy the Zebra.**

**Rex**   Wow   that is one vote for Ziggy   the crowd is going wild

**Iggy**   Yes, yes  no rest here  we have Father Time  strolling up to the front of the stage and turns over his card     **Bronx Bob** *Ohhh-hhh*  my goodness, we are tied this is unbelievable unbelievable.

**Rex**   Mother Nature now holds the fate of each contestant in her hands.   We understand she has just ordered     **ostrich pate** with **olive** branches      along with some **tongue** depressors and **pop tarts** to be in her dressing room    after she turns over her card.

**Iggy**   Her handlers the **four** seasons, are **scurrying** off in all directions to put these into her dressing room so as not to disappoint the *finicky Princess of Nature*.   Both Contestants are waiting with **bated** breath and seem a little  nervous or pissed off   I can't tell from this angle?

**Rex**   Bated breath is that the same as bad breath yet comes with a **hook**?

**Iggy**   Come on Rex, **no** hook    Mother Nature has just walked to the front of the stage, looks at the two contestants, **adjusts** her bra, **blinks** two times, **touches** her right **thigh** looks at her **teeth** in a small **mirror**, and turns over the card ......

**Rex Iggy   ZIGGY THE ZEBRA**

**Iggy**   *Woooow*   intense..... I think the judges got it right Rex got it right Rex   Got it right.

**Rex**   I agree I agree, Iggy How about the *power* of the **Zebra Man**? He's a *force* of nature who's nature  Ziggy Zebra Nature.

**Iggy**   ZZN is the new **Chanel # ZZN**   smell like a Zebra Man.

**Rex**   This won't take long before this **Zebra** is going to be a household fragrance.

**Iggy**   It looks like Ziggy has gone over to **console** Bronx Bob, who looks **visibly** upset.

**Rex**   You don't say  the crowd is going nuts  and the two contestants are saying a few words.

**Iggy**   hopefully words of encouragement.

**Rex**   To think Bronx Bob  was the one who initiated this whole event this week is **mind** dumbing.

**Iggy**   yes, and now he is **embarking** on a new adventure where no man has gone before.

**Rex**   Stunning turn of events it's simply stunning. We have just been informed the other three members of Bronx Bob's team will be **accompanying** Bronx on the rocket for **bye-bye** how would you like to be on that flight.

**Iggy**   They are now transporting **Bob** and his **teammates** over to the rocket. We will try to get a **word** from Bronx before he and his team board the rocket.

**Rex**   I have our winner **Ziggy** here with me. How do you feel about your stunning win?

**Ziggy Zebra** Wow no words can describe how I am feeling. A sh**out out** to Bronx for his great effort and being **my mentor** yet new times are here. I can now work with Mother Earth Mother Nature and Father Time to complete the vision for the planet.

**Iggy** You are a true **inspiration** for all the Entities throughout this planet on what you are **capable** as an Entity.

**Rex** Yes, and you smell great as a **ZEBRA MAN.**

**Iggy** Can you tell us the words you and Bronx exchanged after the announcement?

**Ziggy Zebra** Yes, he wished me well he was very courteous, and I told him he could **conquer** any world he lands on with or without oxygen.

**Rex** If anyone can figure it out

**Iggy** it will be Bronx Bob he's a fighter.

**Rex** Ziggy The Zebra go and finish your life's work.

**Iggy** Ziggy what is that you do again? More specifically, what do you grow that everyone wants?

**Ziggy Zebra** You see Rex and Iggy I'm the real gardener, not **hidden** behind the **scenes**. I take what Mother Earth and Mother Nature have **provided** and turn it into **products** that Homo Sapiens love. So I teach all the entities I can find and set up **territories** for them to **distribute** all under the watchful eye of the *sun*, the *moon*, and the *stars.*

**Iggy** Yes, I get it now Ziggy, good luck to your future.

**Rex** So what does he do, Iggy?

**Iggy** I have no idea ohh, it looks like we have Meco by the MFXY Chromosome Rocket. Meco, how does everything look for the start of this Rocket in the next few moments?

**Meco**   We have gone through all the **bad boy** tests. The Rocket is **burping** and letting a little **gas** out just for **good** measure, yet my brother Seco and I believe we have finally achieved **Rocket Coherency**.

**Rex**   So the rocket has a **consciousness**.

**Meco**   No, it has **gas!**

**Iggy**   You are a true *Rocket Man Meco*   can you get a quick word from Bronx before he and his team board the rocket?

**Meco**   Bronx Bob has just arrived.   Hey, Bronx Bob if you always get what you **want,** and you get what you **need,** what is it that you want or need **right** now?

**Bronx Bob**   Meco, you are asking quite a good question on the heels of one of the first times I have ever lost in my life. What I need right now is one of those **money** machines that count the bills one at a time because where I'm going, I'm going to make a **bloody** fortune.

**Meco**   Bronx, I **love** your enthusiasm.

**Bronx**   Yes, I also want an **endless** supply of green **tea** helps me concentrate a couple of **honeycombs** and some ant **spray** just in case. Yes, also some concrete **powder** to build a **wall** and maybe a **cow** for some **cheese.**

**Meco**   Dip your head Bronx. I am now closing the lid on the capsule.

**Rex**   Wow, he sounds a little **disillusioned** I mean, we can send him those things on a **supply** mission in the future   yet where are you going to **park** the cow?

**Iggy**   Park the cow, where are you going to put the **droppings?** No offense to   **Matilda The Singing Cow** and her offerings last time   they were large chocolate cakes **all stuff no fluff.**

**Rex**   Meco, we are going to turn it over to you for the start of the MFXY Chromosome Rocket.

**Meco**   Thanks, boys I am just going over to the rocket right now we have a *three-phase* system in place this week for the starting procedure. **First,** we open the **latch** where the starter is, **Second** we light the **wick,** which starts the starting gears, and **Third,**   I **run** like **hell** as **far** away as I **can** from the **rocket** before it **ignites.** Here we go   start the countdown
**10 9 8 7 6 5 4 3 2 1**

**Engine trying to start**

**Rex**   wow   it sounds like it is acting up again.

**Iggy**   No, I Think it has too much **gas**   that is why the shaft has puffs of smoke coming out the sides and from the top.

**Rex**   Can you smell the gas or **smoke?** I hope it's not going to *blow* it self *up* or *pout?*

**Iggy**   I think it's bad   gas   or the **eggs** we had for **breakfast** hold on, I think we are having easy over *ohhhhhhhh......*

**Rex**   Liftoff   we have lift off   the **Big s**hiny **shaft** of a rocket has just cleared the big **hands** of the **erector**   and is heading for outer space   *Godspeed   Bronx Bob speed*   may your travels be filled with   *Prosperity speed*   and if you have aches and pains *Grapeseed.*

**Iggy**   Yes Rex, that **stuff** really works!   This has been one hell of a ride this week   and to think it is Bronx Bob   on that rocket, I still can't believe it.   Meco, we heard a few **discrepancies** from the rocket   anything we have to worry about for next week's show?

**Meco**   You know Iggy   a rocket is like a **lover**   sometimes they can be **fun** and **loving**   other times they will **rip** your **heart** out and then, like today, they can **fart** under the **covers**.

**Rex**   Wow, that is why you are called the Rocket Man. I see you managed to **outrun** the flames coming from the rocket.

**Meco**   Seco and I   did a lot of work on the **calculations** on how fast I would have to run after the engine was lit.

**Iggy**   Hey, that was awesome   I think it was the last-minute dive into that **predetermined** hole   that saved your eyebrows.

**Meco** Yes Iggy   I brought an **extra** pair of eyebrows just in case I got a **cramp** in my **leg**   and couldn't **run** as **fast**.

**Iggy**   We will see you next week Meco with a brand new rocket.

**Rex**   Any chance we are going to get a **sneak peek** on the new **sport-themed** Rockets soon.

**Meco**   We are in the testing phase right now   if we can figure out why the **catcher's mitt** keeps throwing the rocket onto the ground in celebratory fashion   then it will be ready for **prime time**.

**Iggy**   Good Luck, Meco. It looks like we are at the end of this show Rex and what a show it was.

**Rex**   Yes Iggy, this was one competition and one week for the ages.

**Iggy**   We'll I guess **two** words will **sum** up this **night**

**Rex Iggy   After party   till we meet again**

**Q the tiny Ukulele.**

**Tiny Ukulele**

Homo Sapien Bob face the world world world
Homo Sapien Bob face the world world world
Homo Sapien Bob face the world world world
Homo Sapien Bob face the world world world

Homo Sapien Bob face the world world world
Homo Sapien Bob face the world world world
Homo Sapien Bob face the world world world
Homo Sapien Bob face the world world world

# AFTERWORD

We Homo Sapiens have been running the planet for the last two hundred thousand years of unending growth and we are precisely where we should be in the hierarchy of life? We're the **kings** of our jungle, and hold the **pinnacle** of power here on earth.

In the enormity that is the universe with it's billions of galaxies and trillions of stars we're just a dust particle on top of a dust particle tucked inside our own solar system three rocks from the sun. I feel like I just let the air out of the baloon I was holding.

Homo Sapien Bob vs the World is a breath of fresh air a funny way to look at the world. Laughing at ourselves as Homo Sapiens and realizing we share this world with Earth Entities. One big happy family! The air is definetly going back into the baloon.

The only problem is Earth Entities have been **evolving** for millions if not billions of years. Homo Sapiens have been evolving for...... well maybe we need a little more time and direction before we can understand our existence? Air slowly starting to escape.

All of Mother Earth's creations and Entities live in the ultimate co-operation. If they can't evolve into their next creation they become extinct. Sounds simple!

We Homo Sapiens on the other hand have all this power and haven't quite figured out what to do with it yet. Stay *on the planet*, blow ourselves up *on the planet,* or move to a *new planet.*

In my first book **Episode One   Bob vs Carl the Coal** I explored a world through the eyes of Carl the Coal. A fun loving coal that loved his family and wanted to do what was best for the world. After three rounds of competition with Bob you got a real sense that Carl brought an energy to the planet.

Bob from Bakersfield California was a family and business man with a great love for life. In his world he saw everything through his rose colored glasses, so he became blind to the realities of life.

Episode Two   **Bronx Bob vs Ziggy the Zebra** is an extension of the same theme expressed in episode one. Bronx Bob works in **between** the laws that govern the people and Ziggy the Zebra works **with** the laws that govern the Universe. Bronx is **fighting with life** and Ziggy is **working with life.**

We Homo Sapiens need to be better observers and not get caught up in the things we cannot control. Earth Entities can be our greatest teachers. We just need to become better students.

Each episode of Homo Sapien Bob vs the World is designed to be a wild and crazy ride in all directions. A reader should be scratching their head thinking how do we go from timpani player to Batman to zonkey to slothing to thrusters to our very own **Meco** Rocket man.

**Rex and Iggy** from *World Mastermind Headquarters* are the glue that binds *Mother Earth Mother Nature and Father Time* together to get their message out to the the planet. They are fun loving yet display signs of brillance, nonsense, comical, and down right off the wall thinking.

As an author **Homo Sapien Bob vs the World** is all about freedom of the mind. Taking a group of characters and ideas for a wild ride through the dimensions of thought. With words and music I get to create a world I desire with an outcome as a snapshot of time.

Hey the air is back in the baloon.

My next book in the series Homo Sapien Bob vs The World  will be another exercise of the mind which should be out late march 2021.

Cheers **Brian Jones**

# ABOUT THE AUTHOR

## Brian Jones

I live in Thailand with my Wife and Daughter in the province of Buriram. I love the concept of Creation and Growth along with Mastery of your Mind and Health to live your Freedom. This formula is my compass to live to 120. A life can be anything you make it so make it great. Cheers

Brian

# BOOKS
By Brian Jones

Longevity Starts Now
Life Happens now what the FXCK
Homo Sapien Bob Episode One
Stop Growing Old in Life
Thailand the First Ten Years

# Info
brianjones.rocks
bwjmusic@gmail.com

# Soon to be released
Habits 5 book series
Homo Sapien Bob Episode Three
The Weightless Lifestyle

www.ingramcontent.com/pod-product-compliance
Lightning Source LLC
Chambersburg PA
CBHW071955230626
47052CB00014B/1155